INEVITABLE

ONLY AFTER DARK

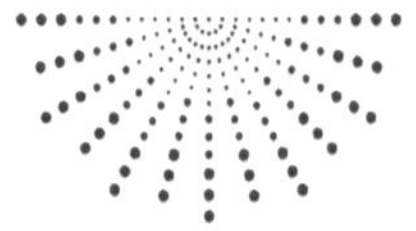

ELLE THORNE

INEVITABLE

ELLE THORNE

Thank you for reading!

*To receive exclusive updates from Elle Thorne and to be
the first to get your hands on the next release,
please sign up for her newsletter.
Put this in your browser:
ellethorne.com*

He's Theo, head of security for Lézare Arceneaux.

He's also Theodoros Ricoletti, son of an Italian lion shifter and his Greek servant woman, raised by the servants in secret until the lion shifter learned he had a son. Theodoros Ricoletti, stolen by his lion shifter father from his servant woman mother, reared by governesses and nannies, sent off to a boarding school, only to run away and join a group of roving shifters.

He's only loved one woman, ever. A beautiful, dark-skinned, glowing-eyed barefooted beauty from the bayou. She betrayed him by casting a spell on him to make him fall in love with another. Just because the spell's been broken doesn't mean that all is healed.

She's Leandra, swamp witch of New Orleans.

She's also Leandra Mathieu, one of the most powerful witches in the surrounding New Orleans. Her ancestors have saved the ass of the Arceneaux Clan more than once. Now, so has she. But she bears secrets. And blood ties.

She shouldn't have fallen for a shifter. She shouldn't have cast the spell on him to make him fall in love with another, either. She has paid enough. Or has she?

Visit ElleThorne.com to sign up for Elle's newsletter!

THE BEGINNINGS

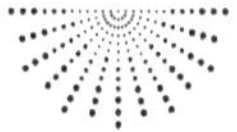

Almost Two Decades Ago

Outside the boundaries of
Black Glade Bayou, Louisiana

"Mémé, I don't want to go to New Orleans to see her," Leandra told her grandmother, Latrice Mathieu.

"She's your mother, *chère*."

"Then why did she drop me off with you and never comes to see me? Why does it feel like she can't wait to leave when we go meet her in the café?"

Mémé shook her head, braids secured to her scalp, her dark skin glowing in the sunlight, her profile majestic.

Leandra glanced in the mirror and studied her preteen features. The dark skin. Her full lips, her eyes—eerie and glowing.

She cast her gaze down. The mirror was her enemy. It reminded her of everything she was that she didn't want to be: The light glowing eyes that betrayed her witch heritage—a sign of the Mathieu witches. The dark skin that boasted of her slave heritage—and the reason her mother rejected her.

Mémé ran her fingertips over Leandra's loose hair. "Let me put this up for you."

"Why? To make *her* happy? To appease her? In case her gentleman or one of his friends might see us?"

Mémé tsked. "You're too wise for one so young."

Too wise.

When Leandra wasn't much older than a toddler, Rochelle, Leandra's mother, had left her with Latrice, her own mother, the one Leandra called Mémé. She'd left her, and yet she'd stayed in town— in New Orleans, living with the gentleman who wouldn't give her his name but was more than happy to provide Rochelle with the trimmings of a high society life.

This was provisional of course. It depended on Rochelle not flaunting her roots.

It wasn't her witch roots that worried him as much as it was her slave roots. No, the gentleman never said as much, but Rochelle knew he prized her for her lighter skin.

Oh, yes, even as a child, Leandra knew. She knew

what it was her mother did. She knew why her mother did it. She was no stranger to life, the impact of skin color, and the carnal nature of mankind.

Though, thanks to Mémé's security, Leandra had never been exposed to the ugly side of carnality. She'd been sheltered from the decisions her mother had made at fourteen, leading her to a life far from their home in the bayou, far from the coven she should have been a part of, far from Mémé's protectiveness.

"Ouch."

Mémé was running a brush through Leandra's unruly curls. "One moment more." She gave it a final swipe. "Now. Let me style this into something that doesn't make you look like a swamp rat."

Leandra was torn between giggling at Mémé's terminology and snarling at her for making her more presentable for Rochelle.

Rochelle, because she couldn't bring herself to call her "mother."

"Mémé, can we go already?" The sooner they went, the sooner they'd get it over with and Leandra could return home to Mémé's cabin in the swamp and take off the shoes that hurt her feet and the dress that restricted her breathing with its high collar.

"We're going, *ma belle*. Relax."

Leandra harrumphed.

To which her grandmother responded with a playful smack.

"Mémé!" Leandra whirled around. "I'm too old for spankings."

"You'll never be too old for spanking, *ma chère*."

MÉMÉ'S GRIP on Leandra's hand was tight. She squeezed her fingers like a cottonmouth taking a frog hostage in the bayou.

Maybe it's because she knows I'm half a heartbeat away from running out of here.

"Here" was the coffee shop they met Rochelle at, on those rare occasions when Rochelle could make time to meet them. It was almost always right after dusk, and Rochelle invariably kept her face in the shadows. Every so often, candlelight would flicker just right and Leandra would get a glimpse of her mother's pale ethereal beauty.

Leandra plopped into the plush chair in the back of the coffee shop, a private room reserved for them when they met with Rochelle. She wondered what the room was used for when they weren't in it. Was it for private assignations? Her mind liked to wander to all sorts of subterfuge, political or amorous. She knew her grandmother would chastise her for her thoughts, but Leandra couldn't help her vivid imagination.

Mémé snapped her fingers, indicating for Leandra to sit up. "You're growing into a young lady, stop acting like a street urchin that's never been taught manners, *chère*."

"Yes, ma'am," Leandra uttered reluctantly and pulled her spine straight.

She felt her mother enter the building. She felt her every time. Was it because of their bond? Was it because of the witch blood they shared, even though Rochelle refused to lay claim to the craft of witchery? Or was it something else, some strange preternatural sense Mémé hadn't explained to her yet? Mémé had begun some of Leandra's sorcery training, but they'd not gotten very far. Mémé said next year would be the year they'd start in earnest.

Sure enough, Leandra's senses were spot-on. A figure appeared in the doorway, pushing aside the curtains that afforded some privacy.

Tall, willowy, with cream-colored skin, attired in the latest fashion, with nails buffed to a high gloss, and hair gleaming, Rochelle Mathieu, mother to Leandra, stood in the doorway.

"*Mère*." Rochelle used the French word for mother.

Leandra fought the sneer wanting to appear on her face at the airs Rochelle put on.

"Rocky." Mémé used the childhood nickname for Rochelle. She took Rochelle's fingers between her weathered hands. "You look wonderful, *chère*. Like life is agreeing with you."

Rochelle's caustic gaze traveled up and down Leandra. "I wish we could say the same for Leandra. She looks like a field hand."

"Those days are long gone," Leandra reminded the woman who'd given birth to her.

"I'm older than you think." Rochelle's tone was haughty, her brow arched high in an unlined, creamy forehead. "So those days are still fresh in my mind."

Her eyes narrowed as she stared at Leandra, taking in her hair—which Leandra was sure had become disheveled in the New Orleans humidity, taking in the scuff marks on the borrowed shoes—because Leandra would rather be barefooted on any given day.

Rochelle held up a bag made of satin material, and fished a tiny jar out. "Here." She handed the jar to Mémé. "Apply this to her skin every night. The smell isn't great, but she'll lose that horrible shading. It will lighten her skin to a beautiful cream color." Rochelle ran the back of her hand along her own cheek, as if this would be the result.

Leandra cocked her head, studied the woman who'd given birth to her, but couldn't seem to like her the way she was. "I'm not—"

Mémé's hand fell heavily on Leandra's shoulder. "Hush, *chère*."

"But—"

"Shall we have sweets?" Mémé interrupted Leandra, giving her a warning look.

"I have early dinner plans. Unforeseen." Rochelle's countenance wasn't apologetic.

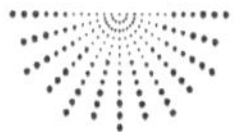

Island of Syros, Greece

Theodoros jumped from rock to rock on the jetty on Syros, the Greek island he lived on with his mother. His agility was something she'd urged him to hide.

As were his other shifter skills.

"Don't let them ever see you as a lion, *agape mou.*" My love. These were the words of caution his mother had preached at him every day since he could remember. Well, every day since the day he'd shifted in front of a stranger when they'd gone to the mainland.

His mother had taken him to Athens, and when a man had stepped too close to her, Theo's protective instincts had flared and he'd begun to morph into his lion.

His mother had thrown her shawl over him and carried little Theo far away from the horrified, stuttering man before he could bring any attention to the little boy who'd grown whiskers and fangs.

Later, she'd held him on a park bench, fed him Greek cookies, and told him he was to never, ever let anyone see him do anything that *normal* little boys couldn't do.

A preteen now, he found it easier to control his urges, easier to control his lion, and easier to control his lion-shifter skills. Sure, he could run faster, jump higher, longer, and out wrestle other boys his age, but now he knew how to control these things.

So, to all eyes on the island of Syros, he was an average little boy, son of a widow woman.

His mother told him his father was a god, he was born of a god and he wasn't allowed to tell anyone. If he was ever asked, he was simply to respond that his father had been a fisherman who'd been lost at sea.

He jumped to the final boulder at the end of the jetty and studied the blueness of the ocean.

One day I'll go farther than this island. One day I'll see more of the world.

And one day, he'd take care of his mother. She toiled in the homes of the wealthy on the island, working hard to provide for herself and her son. She had no social life, no pleasures, no love.

All she had was Theo. Everything she did centered around Theo and his needs.

Yes, for sure, one day this boy would take care of the woman who'd dedicated her life to him.

He looked out over the sea. Why else would he have the skills he had? Was his father Poseidon? What about Zeus?

A part of him mocked his own ideas. How could his father be a Greek god? Another part of Theo wondered how he could take the form of a lion if his father wasn't a god.

The crisp blueness of the ocean burned bright. The fishing boats dotted the horizon. Theo dug deep into his pocket, pulling out the bread and feta his mother had stuffed into plastic wrap. He took fishing line and a hook out. Sure his mother meant for him to eat the feta and bread, but part of it would be bait for the fish near the rocks. Taking a pinch of bread and feta, he rolled it into a tiny ball then pierced it with the hook.

His mother would be happy to see some fresh fish this afternoon. She'd make their favorite fish soup with fresh lemons.

He dropped the hook into the water.

Hours later, it was almost sundown, and Theo had a handful of fish on a line to take home.

He shoved his line and hook in his pocket, wiped his hands on his pants, then dropped to one knee to take the fish from the water where they were strung on a line.

Rising and turning swiftly, he almost ran into a mountain of a man.

He peered up at the man, surrounded by a halo of the setting sun.

Dark haired and tan, the man's black eyes gleamed. A smile crept to his face then spread to his lips, revealing even white teeth.

A slight shiver ran down Theo's spine as he recognized the look of a predator in the man's smile and eyes.

"Theodoros." The man's smile grew larger.

Theo paused. No one called him that. Everyone called him Theo. Even his mother. She only called him Theodoros when he was in trouble. And those times were rare.

He gazed at the man warily, not answering his question. Theo's mother had warned him not to talk to strangers. He wasn't going to break her rules.

"Theodoros Ioannis Ricoletti." The man's smile grew broader.

Young Theo couldn't control his temper and broke his mother's rule. "That's not my name. My name is Theodoros Ioannis Adamantides."

"Adamantides is your mother's last name," the man stated.

"So?"

"Your father is Marco Ricoletti."

"I've never heard that name," Theo scoffed.

"Because your mother took you from your father's home before you were born. She tried to keep you a secret."

Lies.

But then again, was it? His mother never said anything about Theo's father, other than he was a god. Theo knew deep down, that wasn't true. He also knew his mother was holding something back.

"No," he denied the man's statement, though he had no clue if it were true or not.

"No?" The man's grin was predatory, white teeth glistening in the sunset.

A slight crunching sound, and the sound of sinew tearing accosted Theo's senses.

He knew that sound. Knew it only too well from when he'd occasionally snuck an opportunity to shift after his mother went to bed.

The man's face grew broader, his mouth opening wider than a yawn to reveal the lion's erupting canines.

And just as quickly, before his shift could be complete, and before he shifted enough for anyone on the shore to see, the man became completely human.

"You've never seen one of our kind, I suppose." The man's tone held compassion.

"I don't know what you're talking about," Theo blustered.

He lowered himself and stared Theo in the eyes. In the depth of the man's dark gaze, a golden glow blazed. "Of course, you do. You don't want to know."

Theo shook his head adamantly, with the fierce conviction of youth. He stepped around the man and began jumping from boulder to boulder, careful not to slip, while from one hand, the catch of fish dripped. He deliberately made a point not to look back, not to show his fear or vulnerability to this man.

Theo's vulnerability was new to him. He'd always felt safe with the knowledge he could hold his own because, if worse came to worse, he could always shift into his lion and take care of himself regardless of circumstance. But this lion-shifter man would be a larger lion. And Theo recognized his own lion wouldn't be able to take the man's lion. This was the first time fear gripped him. Of course, not that Theo would easily give in to the temptation to shift. He wouldn't. No way he'd disobey his mother if it could be avoided.

He peered down the distance of the jetty. At the

very start of it, at the almost-deserted docks, stood a handful of men.

All of them were large.

All of them had a predator's confident stance.

Shifters. All.

Now, he couldn't help a glance at the man.

"Those are yours?" Theo nodded toward the waiting team.

The man nodded. "I'd like you to go with me."

"Go where?"

"Home."

"Your home?"

"Your home, too."

Theo froze in his tracks. He gave the man his hardest glare. "Explain."

"I'm Marco Ricoletti."

Theo tried to absorb the man's revelation.

He's my father.

He studied the man with the Italian name. "No." He shook his head. "That's not true."

"You know it is."

Deep down, Theo did. He let out a long, ragged breath. "I can't go to your home." He knew the man's home couldn't be on Syros. Wherever this man lived, it wasn't on this island. And it wasn't where his mother would be.

"I've scoured the earth, looking for you. Your

mother had no right to take you away. No right to keep my son from me."

Confusion swirled in Theo's mind like a tornado's funnel. This grown-up stuff was more than he could wrap his head around.

"You're coming with me." The man's quiet assurance brooked no argument.

And yet, Theo couldn't comply. "I can't."

"For the sake of your mother's life, you'd be better off coming. I can leave word with her you'll be staying with me."

"No." The word was released with his lion's snarl. Theo's lion pushed against his mind, pressing for a shift, pushing for the opportunity to react to this man's arrogance. "Do not threaten my mother."

Marco Ricoletti released a low chuckle. "You're a fierce one."

Theo heard the sound a fraction of a second too late. Before he could react, half a dozen pairs of hands had grabbed him and placed a hood over his head.

A slight pinch in his arm was the last thing he felt.

MORE BEGINNINGS

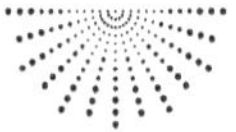

Almost a Decade Ago

CHAPTER THREE

Milan, Italy

Theo had never been able to call him father, even though he'd been in Milan for years, living in the same home as Marco.

Marco had told him, originally, he'd made arrangements with his mother to join them in Italy. They lived in a villa larger than several homes put together.

Not believing Marco was taking steps to bring his mother to him, Theo had asked daily to see her. Marco repeatedly told him that one day he would. That day didn't come soon enough for the impatient youth.

So, he ran away.

Marco found him and brought him back.

He ran away again.

And again.

And again.

And each time, using his tracking skills to find Theo, Marco brought him back.

"Why do you keep bringing me back?" a distraught young Theo had yelled at Marco in desperation.

"I lost Cristiano, my first son. I won't lose you, too."

Finally, one day, not even six months after he'd seen his mother for the last time, Marco brought her to Milan and set her up in a house on the property.

And that was how they'd lived the next few years. Marco staying in the villa, his mother in the little house nearby.

Then, a few years later, much too young to have it happen, Theo's mother died. Marco had paid for a beautiful casket and service, and had her buried in the mountains a few miles north on old Ricoletti family property. While there, Marco showed Theo his own father's and mother's grave.

"There will be a place for me. And one day for you."

Theo never said a word. He never told his father he'd never stay here, never be buried here.

But the next day, still in his teens, he left a note for his father and hopped on a bus.

He'd spent years with the man who'd sired him. Marco had provided everything a man could want in terms of education. Fine arts, martial arts, and shifter skills. And though Theo had no problem with his father, the powerful, wealthy lion shifter. But Italy was not Theo's home.

Nor was Greece.

Theo felt homeless, anchorless.

He struck out for America.

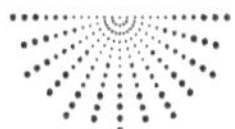

CHAPTER FOUR

Black Glade Bayou, Louisiana

Leandra didn't own a black dress to wear to the funeral. She found one to wear in the back of Mémé's closet. The irony of having to borrow one of Mémé's black dresses to wear to Mémé's funeral didn't sit well with Leandra.

But it's not like I'm going to go to town to buy one.

No. Leandra wouldn't go to town to get a dress. She didn't go to town at all. Mémé was the one who went to town for supplies.

Who's going to do that now?

Leandra shrugged, though she was having a conversation with herself, inside her own mind. She'd find anything she needed for sustenance in the swamp.

She tugged on the dress. It was far too uncomfortable, tight on her hips, tight on her breasts.

She cursed her curviness.

Then again, there was so much about herself Leandra had cursed over the years. The dark skin that displeased her mother. The curly, unruly hair that she refused to do much with.

Brush your hair, you look like a street urchin, Mémé had said countless times before she passed.

I should brush it, if only for Mémé's funeral.

It would make her grandmother happy, wherever she was watching from.

Leandra picked up her grandmother's brush but didn't move the shawl that covered the mirror's reflective surface.

Leandra never did use the skin bleaching cream Rochelle gave to Mémé. The stench of the cream made her nose crinkle. She'd tossed the open jars, one by one, into the bayou.

She'd also refused to ever see Rochelle again. And Mémé had given up trying to force Leandra to leave the bayou to see her mother.

They'd pursued her education in sorcery. Mémé had become the mother Leandra had never had, and she'd never said a word when Leandra draped her shawls over the two mirrors in the cabin. But she did take the shawls down.

They'd hardly discussed Rochelle after Leandra

became a teen, and Leandra remained the wild child witch that lived in the swamp with her Mémé, learning the skills of the Black Glade Coven and staying away from vampires because vampires could kill a fledgling witch.

Leandra met Tante Lucia once, when she'd returned to New Orleans and joined Leandra, Rochelle, and Mémé at the café at dusk.

Tante Lucia had sat in one corner of the room, studying Rochelle with a gaze that sparked with ill-concealed anger.

With a final jerk on the brush, Leandra picked up Mémé's shoes that she'd have to borrow as well. She'd walk barefoot until she arrived at the cemetery so as not to ruin Mémé's shoes in the swamp.

Might as well get to the funeral.

MÉMÉ WAS BEING BURIED in the cemetery outside the Black Glade community hall, and that was just around the bend of the path following the bayou. Leandra paused to put on Mémé's shoes.

She'd definitely need to steel herself in preparation for the witches that would be at Mémé's funeral. Leandra was sure some of them wouldn't be sad.

Who would? She wanted to tick the names off in

her mind, but all she could concentrate on was the pinching of her shoes.

"Well, if it isn't Leandra Mathieu, joining us at her grandmother's funeral. I'm surprised you could leave your frogs and other swamp creatures long enough to honor your grandmother." The voice was snide and cold, both at the same time.

"Adelise." Leandra turned, though she didn't need to. She knew that voice. It had followed her whenever she was in the vicinity of the Black Glade coven.

It hadn't always been this way between Leandra and Adelise. Once, long ago, Leandra had thought of her as a friend, until Adelise's mother convinced Adelise the two best friends were in competition for the coveted coven leadership.

Little did they know, Leandra had no interest in heading up the coven.

Sure, leading the coven had fallen under the purview of the Mathieu family, but that changed after Mémé had disqualified herself years ago. Circumstances kept the leadership from Lucia, and as for Rochelle, she wanted nothing to do with witches, that was no secret.

And now there was Leandra.

And I don't give a shit about the hierarchy of the coven and who leads them.

Leandra put on a sticky sweet smile. "Adelise,

would you like to be one of my swamp frogs?" She cocked her head, studying Adelise's fearful expression. "No, I think you'd be better off as a swamp rat." Leandra raised her hands, flicked her fingers as if readying to cast a spell. "Scurry away little rat."

"You wouldn't dare. The coven... My mother... The ..." She sputtered, out of words.

"You know better."

You bet your ass Leandra would put a spell on another witch. In a heartbeat. Except there was still a memory, of Adelise, of being close friends. That loyalty kept Leandra's ire at bay.

"Leandra, I'm glad you could make it." Michelina scrutinized her.

Why wouldn't I be here? Leandra bit her tongue.

"We're going to be calling a meeting sometime soon. Decisions have to be made."

Not by me.

"No problem."

As if she'd bother showing up. There was no good reason to be in attendance, was there?

A throat clearing behind her made Leandra turn slowly. Now who would she have to deal with?

"You shouldn't be here, Lucia." Michelina stated.

"I shouldn't be at my own mother's funeral?" Lucia, not looking a day older than the first and last time Leandra saw her.

"Tante Lucia." She studied the dark-haired, light-eyed woman. A golden flicker in the depth of her eyes showed Leandra her shifter animal. A white tiger shifter, that much Leandra did know.

"Leandra." Lucia put her fingertips on Leandra's shoulders.

A current ran from those fingers throughout Leandra's body. Was that the effect of her shifter animal, or was it because of the witch's blood coursing through Lucia?

"How are you doing, little one?" Concern settled on Lucia's face, her gaze unwavering.

Lucia's kindness made tears flood Leandra's eyes. "I miss her."

"I know you do. I do, too. Let's get through this then go somewhere. Lunch, maybe." She looked around. "Rochelle is not here?"

Leandra shook her head. That wasn't exactly a shocker.

A dangerous gleam appeared in Lucia's eyes. "My sister…" She didn't finish her sentence, shaking her head instead.

ATTENDANCE AT LATRICE MATHIEU—MÉMÉ'S—FUNERAL was high. The service was short.

Leandra knew that would be exactly how Mémé

would have wanted it. She was never much for formality.

"Let's visit Quake. Have lunch, maybe a latte and some beignets? They have the very best in town."

"How can you think about food at this time?" The words slipped out of Leandra before she could put her filter in place.

She was ready to apologize, except Lucia raised her hand and released a low laugh.

"My mother said you were just like her. I see that's so."

"I'll take that as a compliment." Leandra was angry laughter could slip past Lucia's lips on a day like this.

"Don't be angry with me. My mother had a full wonderful life. She lived longer than some witches, not as long as others. She knew it was time to go. She'd done her job."

"What do you mean?" Leandra glanced at the dark-haired woman in black.

"We'll talk at Quake."

"But—" Leandra began a protest.

"No." Lucia's hand went up. The only thing she didn't do was say *talk to the hand.*

Thank goodness, Leandra thought

The drive to New Orleans went quick, though it wasn't all that short.

"I've missed going to Quake," Lucia confessed.

"Where have you been that you couldn't go?" Leandra asked.

Lucia gave her a sideways glance. "Quake."

That's all she said.

Fine. We'll talk at Quake.

Leandra stayed silent for the rest of the trip, but she'd picked up a slight hint of emotion behind the singular word Quake when Lucia had said it.

What's that about?

CHAPTER FIVE

New Orleans, Louisiana

Lucia parked the car in front of the restaurant —although a weathered, battered old sign clearly proclaimed this was a no parking zone.

Leandra pointed to the sign. "You could get towed."

"They wouldn't dare."

The tone in Lucia's voice gave Leandra pause. She so wanted to delve into the topic, but Lucia's face was as welcoming as a cottonmouth's.

"What is this place?" Leandra studied the building, with its balconies, standard for New Orleans.

Balconies laced with metal architecture over each door and in front of windows on the second floor created the illusion there were several buildings, not once giving a hint the original structures had been fitted into one building. Not many knew Quake occupied the entire block—a secret known only to the paranormal beings that inhabited the area.

The entrances were marked with different colored doors; the walls were dilapidated.

Lucia halted in the middle of the sidewalk between two buildings. This brought Leandra to a full stop next to her.

She looked at her aunt. "What's up, Tante?"

"Just taking a moment." Lucia inhaled a deep breath then released it slowly.

"What is it?" She studied her aunt, so starkly beautiful, curves emphasized by a dark mourning dress.

One last exhale, then Leandra put a smile on her face as if it was a difficult task. "Nothing. Let's go in. You're familiar with the doors, the rules, all that?"

Leandra had heard rumors, but she would welcome the opportunity to hear more. Quake had a mysterious reputation in the witch world. A restaurant that doubled as a meeting place for supernatural beings.

Yeah, who wouldn't want to hear more?

Especially when she'd heard they welcomed all beings, as long as they remained segregated.

"Not really," she told Lucia. "Tell me, Tante?"

Lucia nodded. "Shifters come here, and vampires

and witches and elementals. Other types at times. Shifters use the blue door. The red is for witches. The green for vampires. Black for elementals."

"Which do you use? Born of a witch, but you're a shifter."

"What do you know of my heritage, Leandra?"

"Mémé didn't want to say much, Tante."

Lucia nodded. "Quake has rules. No interactions with types other than your own. No fighting between types, species, or individuals. And no questions about Quake."

"No problem," Leandra acquiesced.

"I'm surprised my mother never brought you here."

"I don't like coming to town. Mémé didn't force me."

Lucia began a forward trek toward the red door. "You'll have to tell me what your plans are. Surely you can't stay in the cabin on the swamp."

Why can't I?

Leandra wasn't going to ask her, but she could imagine nothing else she'd rather do.

Lucia opened the red door.

"Why this door?"

"You're not a shifter. I'm descended from witches."

Leandra accepted the explanation and stepped into a room of floor-to-ceiling black curtains with barely any lighting other than two sconces with candles on the wall to the left and to the right. Across from the door they'd just entered through was another door.

A woman stepped forward, clad in a black gown that matched her ebony hair. Her skin appeared luminescent. Leandra tried to study her without being obvious she was doing so.

The woman gave off preternatural vibes but wasn't a witch, and nor was she a shifter.

Her face was a forbidding mask, unwelcoming, though she was supposed to be a hostess, or at least that was what Leandra assumed.

"Lucia." A smile appeared on the woman's unemotional countenance. "I'm not sure where to seat you."

"Where you always used to."

"He'd kill me if I did."

Leandra glanced from one to the other. What was this about?

Lucia rolled her eyes. "Witch section, then, but the room closest to the shifters, if you don't mind. I'll feel more comfortable closer to my own kind."

"Absolutely. I've missed you." The stoic hostess wrapped her arms around Lucia.

Leandra picked up Lucia's discomfort with the touch, but her aunt didn't move away.

"I've missed you, too, Bethany."

Bethany pulled away. "He's missed you, too."

Who the hell is that? Who is he? Leandra glanced at Lucia for answers, but she was avoiding eye contact with her.

I'll get to the bottom of this, sooner or later.

"I don't need to review the rules with you, do I?" Bethany asked.

"Not unless you were told to remind me."

"He doesn't know you're here." Bethany glanced upward. "Yet."

Leandra's gaze followed Bethany's to the black ceiling.

Of course, there was nothing there.

"I'd heard he was out of town. Guess I heard wrong." Lucia gave a one-shouldered shrug.

Leandra reached for Lucia's hand and squeezed her fingers. "What am I missing?" she whispered as low as she could.

Bethany glanced at Leandra, clearly she'd heard.

Lucia shook her head. No answer was coming from her.

Bethany led them down a red-walled corridor marked with doorways every few feet until they'd come to a point where the red ended and turned blue. She made an abrupt left at a doorway and entered the tiny alcove of a room.

The room held three tables, each with two chairs. The tables, as well as the room, were empty. The only lighting was a hurricane lamp on each table. The artwork was subdued and unidentifiable, even with her preternatural vision.

Bethany pulled two black scrolls from a wrought iron latticed holder next to the doorjamb. "As close as I can get you without actually putting you in the shifter section," she explained. "They may accept you, but there's no way they'd be accepting of Leandra.

Leandra did a double take, eyes narrowed.

How the hell does she know my name?

Bethany smiled, as if she knew what was on Leandra's mind. "Enjoy your visit." She set the scrolls on the table.

Lucia took a seat, indicating for Leandra to join her.

Leandra dropped into the velvet covered plush chair, reached for the scroll, and unrolled it. "This is the menu?"

There were no prices, all that was listed were the entrees, appetizers, desserts, and a wine and cocktail selection.

"How do you know how much everything costs?" she asked Lucia.

"There's no cost. Quake picks up the tab."

"For us? Why?"

"No." Leandra opened her own menu. "For everyone."

What kind of place does this?

"So the restaurant pays everyone's tab?"

"No. Quake does."

Leandra cocked her head. "That's the..." She didn't know what else to say.

"This is Quake's place. It's named after him." A slight tremor rolled through Lucia's voice.

Whoa. What's this? How could I not know?

Sure, she lived in the swamp, but she did hear talk. Why didn't she know this?

She studied her aunt. "Tante—"

Lucia glanced down at her menu. "You're no longer a child. Call me Lucia."

Not to mention, she looks young enough to be my sister. Those shifters with their longevity. They managed to age better than witches, and live longer, too.

Leandra nodded. "Lucia, do you know this Quake person?"

"Know him?" The one-shoulder shrug thing again, then, "I used to know him."

Leandra waited for Lucia to continue.

Nothing. Lucia's eyes were glued to the menu. When she glanced up, she said, "So what are your plans?"

"To stay in Mémé's cabin."

"She left it to you in her will. You'll find out at the reading. I won't be there."

"Why did she leave it to me?" Mémé had two daughters after all. "And where will you be?"

"I'm leaving New Orleans. I have no reason to be here. You're the only one she could leave it to. Not me, since she knew I didn't want to stay in town. Not Rochelle."

Leandra didn't need to ask why Mémé wouldn't leave it to her mother. Rochelle would have burned it to the ground. But still, it would have been nice to hear something, anything, from Lucia. Leandra felt as though she'd lived in a vacuum. She barely knew anything about her aunt or her mother. Or even her grandmother's life prior to Leandra's birth.

"Why not Rochelle?"

Lucia fixed her with a pointed stare. "I'd think that was obvious." She rolled the menu back into a scroll. "I'm having the daily special. It's been a long time since I've had decent etouffee. You?" Her tone told Leandra all talk about family was over.

Tears burned Leandra's eyes. Etouffee was her Mémé's specialty. "Same. I'm going to the restroom to wash up." And get rid of the sadness that began to eat at her, knowing she'd be in the cabin.

Without Mémé.

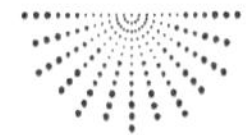

CHAPTER SIX

New Orleans, Louisiana

Theo leaned against the wall at Quake and tried to get control of his lion. He'd seen her walk in. His lion had reacted with such fervor it had pushed Theo close to a shift.

Yeah, that's what I need to do, shift at Quake and start a goddamned supernatural world war.

True that, his lion agreed.

It would not be a good thing.

But that woman.

Fuck.

She'd started a campaign of battles within him. His lion battled with common sense, wanting to approach her. His cock battled with his mind. His nose picked up her scent and let it imprint on his soul, damned near making her a part of him.

How can this be?

His lion roared deep within his head. *She's the one.* He roared the sentiment with vigor and a volume that made Theo want to grab his head.

There's no way to know that, Theo insisted, arguing with himself, with his lion, with his senses, with his soul, with the universe.

He couldn't erase the image of her, though it was a brief glimpse.

Skin the color of mocha, exactly the shade of the beverages Maylene—his boss's housekeeper would make for them every afternoon. A perfect, cream-topped concoction that coursed down his throat, warming him. Yes, this woman he'd seen, she was that same shade and left him with the same warmth.

Warmth, hell. She left him with a hot sensation.

Yeah, hot.

His pants tightened in all the wrong places, for all the right reasons. He was in public for fuck's sake, even though Quake was dimly lit.

He'd seen her, then couldn't go back into the room he was in with Lézare and some of Lézare's business associates. Lézare—his boss.

And best friend.

When Theo first arrived in America, not long ago,

he'd been in New York, roaming the streets, looking for his bearings. He'd chanced an excursion into a territory controlled by the Romanoff polar bear shifters.

One of the Romanoffs, a hotheaded shifter called John, had decided to teach the roaming lion shifter a lesson. He and his group of shifters had chased Theo through the dark alleys.

Yeah, Theo was no fool. There was no way he could take half a dozen polar bear shifters.

He fought them. Bravely. Bloody and aching, he could see the writing on the wall. He couldn't win this battle.

Of course, he got the hell out of there as quick as he could.

Not quick enough.

Or maybe if he'd only known the terrain of the concrete jungle better, he wouldn't have found himself cornered.

But he was cornered.

And so very fucked.

Those polar bear shifters were going to kick his ass. Leave him dead.

But Theo knew he'd take at least one of them with him.

He'd just begun to let his lion take over and shift when he heard a throat clearing behind him.

He'd whirled around, ready to face more polar

bears and wondering how the hell they'd managed to flank him.

Except it wasn't a polar bear. It was a white tiger shifter, dark haired, dark eyed, a mischievous smile on his face.

Theo took an instinctive and instant liking to the man. Something about his tiger connected with Theo's lion.

"John Romanoff. Still the bully, aren' you." The white tiger shifter addressed the polar bear with a drawl that seemed to have a French accent laced throughout, dropping the last consonant, as Theo learned was Lézare's way.

The drawl was lazy, but the man's eyes were predatory.

This white tiger was no one to fuck with.

It didn't hurt that more than a handful of the largest shifters Theo had ever seen stepped forward, out of the darkness, some leaping from fire escapes, landing with feline precision.

The white tiger shifter was accompanied by a variety of animal shifters. Bear. Panther. Wolf. Each of the newly arrived shifters stood behind the white tiger, ready to do battle.

"Lézare Arceneaux," the polar bear shifter called John Romanoff said with a frown. "You're trespassing."

Theo glanced between the two shifters.

The one he'd called Lézare, with the French-tipped Southern drawl released a laugh, dug a phone out of his pocket, and pressed on the screen. He paused, then said, "Mikhail. John's up to his pranks again." He gave the polar bear shifter a glance as if he were talking about a petulant toddler. "I'd hate to have to kick his ass and send him home with his polar bear tail tucked between his legs. Want to talk to your son or…" Lézare arched a brow at John Romanoff. He held his phone up. "Want to talk to your father?"

John Romanoff grunted, then released a low growl from deep within his gut. Without a word, he turned around, a full one-eighty, then sauntered away nonchalantly.

Except the straightness to his spine displayed his agitation.

The white tiger shifter put his phone away and held his hand out to Theo. "Lézare Arceneaux. Though I guess you figured that out."

"Theo Ricoletti." Theo shook Lézare's hand. "Thank you. They had me."

"Maybe. But you'd have taken a few of them down with you. We couldn't let you be taken out though. We watched you handle yourself. Impressive. Where's that accent from?"

Theo released a sigh. He figured the day would come when someone would ask him about his past.

Shifters stayed in packs or found new packs. Being solo like this would raise questions. "Greece. Then Italy."

Lézare nodded. "Interested in a job?"

Theo fought to keep his composure. *Just like that?* "Seriously?" Then suspicion set in. "Doing what?"

"Security. We're in Louisiana. New Orleans." He pronounced it more like N'Awlins, but Theo didn't take long to get accustomed to Lézare's accent.

He didn't take long to get accustomed to anything about Lézare. They'd become tight friends.

Fast forward, and now here he was, security for the Arceneaux clan because he could handle himself in a scuffle.

And that was all thanks to his father, Marco Ricoletti, who'd seen to his education, and part of that included the art of defense and offense.

Today, standing against the wall in Quake, Theo felt Lézare's presence before he saw him. He felt his heartbeat as he approached, recognized his footfall, and waited for Lézare to get close enough.

Lézare stood next to him then leaned against the wall. "Not coming back to the gathering?" He indicated the room with the other shifters in it.

"Just taking a second." How could he possibly explain to his best friend and boss he'd seen a woman and she'd started a chain reaction in him that he needed a few moments to recover from.

Plus, I wouldn't mind catching another look at her. Maybe even a quick hello.

She'd been in the witch section. That should bother him. Theo knew it should. Hell, it should have been a deterrent.

Shifters and witches.

Oil and water.

But still—he released a sigh—that damned chemistry.

"You sure you're okay?" Lézare pushed.

"Fine." Theo had glanced at Lézare when movement caught his attention. He glanced toward the movement.

Her!

His pulse jumped. His heart rammed into his throat at the same time. He couldn't swallow because his damned heart was there blocking his esophagus. Or maybe that was a brick.

Who the hell knew?

He felt eyes on him, glanced at Lézare.

Sure enough, Lézare had locked his gaze on Theo, studying him.

In an instant, Lézare had read him.

Read his reaction.

Read his pulse.

Sensed and maybe even scented his emotions.

Lézare's eyes narrowed, his gaze glued to the woman. "No, Theo."

"No what?" Theo couldn't tear his scrutiny from the curvy figure turning the corner into the ladies' restroom.

"Not her, Theo. Never her. She's…" Lézare shook his head. "Just no. Stay away from the swamp witch." Lézare turned his attention to the room the rest of their party was in. "Coming?"

"In a second."

Lézare shook his head. "Brother, be careful. Keep your distance. Some things shouldn't happen."

Is it because she's a witch?

Theo had questions. Many of them. But he knew Lézare as well as he knew himself. Lézare wasn't interested in covering this matter with him. He was done.

And with that, Lézare left the hallway and reentered the room.

A magnet the size of Texas drew him in as if he were a hapless piece of steel. He made his way toward the restrooms in the red hall. He should have headed toward the blue shifter restrooms. Sure, he knew that. Just as he knew he shouldn't want this woman the way he did.

How did he begin to describe the chemical reaction of this attraction?

He stopped in front of the red men's restroom, hoping no warlocks would exit.

That's all I need. To be caught here.

The ladies' restroom door opened.

Out she slipped. Elegant and with the ease of a panther sliding through the rainforest.

Witch—everything about her screamed witch.

It should have screamed a warning to Theo.

It wouldn't have mattered.

Her eyes drew to him. She studied him briefly, a dilation behind her eerie, light eyes. It was like looking into moonlight.

He was transfixed.

She inhaled a breath, softly.

A sound his shifter hearing had no problem picking up. The sound amplified through his body. Her pulse raised, beginning a tempo that grew ever faster.

"Shifter." The word glided across her lips, the decibel level so low, no human, and even some supernatural beings wouldn't have picked it up— unless they were standing next to her, like Theo was.

He nodded. "Who are you? I have to know."

Just then, he caught the sight of motion in his peripheral vision.

He turned.

Another woman appeared. She resembled this ethereal being Lézare had called a swamp witch.

The newcomer appraised Theo. He returned in kind. She was a mystery. He sensed a witch but saw a shifter in her eyes. Without her making any attempt to mask the shifter within her, he could see it was a white tiger shifter.

And yet, the familial resemblance to the swamp witch was undeniable.

The newcomer put her hand on the other woman's shoulder. "Leandra. Let us go."

Leandra.

His lion roared in Theo's mind, drowning out more than his heartbeat and any thoughts he had.

CHAPTER SEVEN

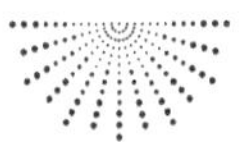

New Orleans, Louisiana

Leandra stared at the swarthy, dark-haired man before her. What was a shifter doing in the red section? His gaze was intense, drawing her in like a whirlpool seduces a piece of driftwood, sucking it in, taking it down, claiming every part of it.

She was lost in his black gaze, dragged farther and farther into the vortex he was creating within her.

Time slipped away as if it were everything—and nothing. She didn't notice Lucia approach until she felt her hand on her shoulder. "Leandra. Let us go."

A roar filled Leandra's head. She put her hand over her ears, trying to push it away, trying to block it out. All to no avail. The sound was not coming from outside her mind.

Leandra didn't want to go.

Lucia's lips were moving, saying something, but the roar drowned it out. The man's eyes pierced her, straight through to her core. Staring into those dark windows to his soul, with the golden glimmer of his lion rampaging within, she felt as if she were looking into a mirror.

Not the mirrors she'd always hated.

No, in this mirror, she saw truth, integrity, beauty, and the blossoming self-assurance that this creature before her wanted her.

The gorgeous hunk of man with his muscular build straining at the fabric of his shirt was overwhelmed by her.

Lucia's hand trailed down to Leandra's fingers where she took them in a tight grasp and pulled her away, back to the table.

And still, with every step she took, she felt the lion shifter's scrutiny on her.

Lucia and Leandra sat at their table. During their absence, two iced teas had been brought to their table, served in frosted glasses, dripping with condensation onto the dark tabletop.

Lucia took a quick sip then jumped into a conversation. "What was that about? Do you know him? He's with the Arceneaux."

Leandra battled the urge to return to the doorway and look for the shifter. "I've never seen him before."

Lucia made a tiny tsk of doubt. "You didn't seem like strangers."

"You haven't answered any of my questions." Leandra raised a brow. Maybe this could convince Lucia to be more forthcoming with information.

Her aunt frowned. "What do you want to know?"

Really? Leandra fought the sarcasm back. "Quake, for starters."

"He's part of my past." The words were clipped, propelled through tightened lips and a clenched jaw.

So that's how it's going to be. Fine, then.

"Alright. Where do you live?"

"Most of the time in Europe."

"Why?"

Lucia heaved a sigh, opened her mouth to speak, then closed it when a woman that could have been Bethany's twin appeared with two plates of etouffee.

"Enjoy," the black-clad server said, without a smile.

Lucia nodded then, as soon as the woman had left, said, "I didn't grow up here. My father is—was— an Arceneaux. A shifter. He came to claim me, taking me to Europe to be raised by one of his relatives."

"And that's where you are now?"

"You're persistent. You get that from your Mémé."

"Did you miss her? Growing up away from her?" Leandra couldn't imagine a life without Mémé.

"Did you miss *your* mother?"

Leandra frowned. "Do you ever answer questions?" she huffed.

Lucia laughed, a sound that carried softly all about the room. It was like hearing a tiny bell.

"I did answer questions."

"Some. And no. How could I miss *her?* Rochelle didn't want me in her life to begin with. She wanted a… I am an embarrassment to her."

"Rochelle has issues."

"I'll say," Leandra scoffed.

"No, it's more than you think. Food's getting cold." Lucia stirred her etouffee.

There was no more conversation that day.

Lucia took Leandra back to the cabin and drove away, down the pebbled road that flooded when the rains were strong enough.

Leandra watched her drive off, then entered the solitude of the cabin, leaving the shawl over the mirror.

THE COURTSHIP

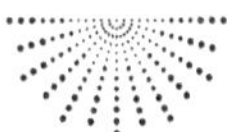

A Handful of Years Ago

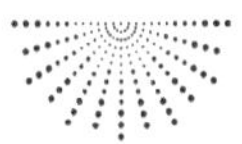

CHAPTER EIGHT

Outside the boundaries of
Black Glade Bayou, Louisiana

Theo stretched his muscular lion limbs. He sniffed at the bayou air, hoping to catch her scent.

Her.

Leandra.

The woman who'd been at Quake.

Nothing.

Last week, on one of his weekly runs—a man had to let his lion have its head every so often—he'd caught her scent on the downward breeze.

It was faint, but his lion knew. The lion had roared, shaking the trees in the swampy water, making the water ripple.

Birds had flown, bayou creatures had scurried. He'd thrown his head back and sniffed harder, taking in so much air his lion chest felt like it was going to burst.

It didn't burst, but his heart was forlorn, because of her.

She'd been in the bayou. Somewhere. Sometime.

Not long ago, and not too far away, else he'd never have been able to catch her delicious scent.

He'd been wanting to find her, hadn't had a chance to look. Working for Lézare kept him on the road, out of town, and, at times, out of the country, while his boss added to his empire. They'd finally settled back in New Orleans on a more permanent basis.

After settling in, the first thing on Theo's mind and his lion's heart had been locating the woman whose scent had seared itself into his memory.

He began a lope, keeping a brisk pace and only stopping to sniff the air and see if her scent was stronger and if he might be closer to finding her.

A new scent infiltrated his senses.

Shifter.

White tiger shifter.

Correction: White tigress! A female shifter was in the bayou's brush.

Theo picked up the scent immediately. Thankful his sense of smell was better than most shifters.

He froze in his tracks, his senses on high alert. Something made the fur on his back stand straight up. The thick muscles on his lion's back and chest tightened and flexed with anticipation that there might be conflict. He knew he was still in Lézare's territory.

Or am I?

Had he pushed himself farther out of Lézare's territory? The area outside the Arceneaux claim was typically populated by non-shifters types. Witches and vampires.

Theo had urged Lézare, at times, to let him push the other types back, to stretch Arceneaux boundaries farther and claim more area, but Lézare staunchly refused. Said it wasn't what his ancestor Étienne had wanted.

Theo didn't pry. He could tell from the set of Lézare's jawline he'd crossed into a topic his boss didn't want to discuss.

Theo sidestepped in his lion form, standing in the shadows of an old cypress tree.

"You think I don't know you're here, lion?" A very definite female voice came from the brush.

Theo shifted quickly, with the twinge of discomfort he'd worked hard to tune out. Morphing wasn't painless, but with enough training and willpower, he'd turned it into more of an acute but short-lived pain than a long drawn out excruciating process.

"I could say the same," Theo countered.

"I'm aware you're cognizant of my presence." A woman stepped from the brush.

He knew her face. The woman who'd been with Leandra at Quake that day.

"I know you."

"And I know you, Theo Ricoletti, security for the Arceneaux Group."

"Your name?"

"Lucia." A tiny smile graced her lips, pulling the corners upward.

It struck Theo again that she bore a great resemblance to Leandra. "Your last name?"

"Last names don't mean much to me."

He nodded. He got that. He'd used his mother's last name. It was his promise to her on her deathbed that he would use Marco's surname. And he had. Reluctantly so.

"You're related to Leandra." Stating the obvious, hoping for an answer. Maybe even Leandra's last name. That'd be a great start.

Not that he'd do anything with the knowledge. It's not like he could go out and ask questions about the dark-skinned, exotic beauty. Lézare would find out and that wouldn't do.

He felt guilty enough about his feelings after Lézare's warning.

"I am." Lucia plucked a long blade of straw-like

grass and rolled it between her fingers. "She's my sister's daughter."

He caught the note when she said sister—definitely a sour note.

"Leandra's a witch." Stating the obvious again. "You're a shifter…"

She nodded. "It's convoluted."

"I'll say, considering how witches and shifters feel about one other."

"There are exceptions." She had a wicked gleam in her eye but, thankfully, not an evil one.

"I'm sure." He narrowed his eyes, trying to figure out where she was going with this.

"You are the exception. Leandra is as well. The attraction between you two isn't possible to hide. It wasn't that day, and it's obvious why you're haunting the bayou, seeking, searching, making your way through the marshes, silently, but ever hopeful."

A chill crossed over his body. He had no idea what he felt was so obvious. But Lucia had said the attraction wasn't possible to hide. Was it two-sided? Did Leandra dream of him nightly as he did of her? She preoccupied his dreams consistently. "What makes you think you know what you're talking about?"

Lucia shook her head. "Sometimes, shifters are so blockheaded." She laughed, as if it was occurring to her she was a shifter herself. "What you and Leandra have…it is inevitable. It could no sooner be denied or avoided than the sunrise's glorious path across an azure morning sky." She flicked the blade of straw, and, as if it were a miniature spear, it sailed through the air and pierced through the marshy under-growth. "You'll go to Quake tomorrow. You'll sit near the same area you saw us that day."

He cocked his head. Who was she to give him orders? Then again, it occurred to him… He had to do it. Something in him, in his lion, too, something wouldn't let him stay away.

"Will you tell me why?"

"It is time to set your destiny in motion. Yours and Leandra's. It was predetermined and seen by others wiser than I am."

He nodded.

"And lion shifter?"

"Yes, Lucia."

"It won't be an easy road you travel with her. But it will be worthy of both of you."

She vanished into the brush. Theo didn't pursue her; he understood the need to slip away unfollowed.

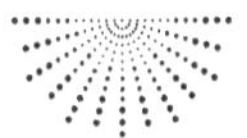

CHAPTER NINE

Black Glade Bayou, Louisiana

Leandra sighed. It was the anniversary of Mémé's death. She'd lost count of the years.

Okay, no she hadn't. She simply didn't want to remember how long since she'd seen Mémé.

Leandra had become accustomed to the solitude of the cabin, only venturing out to attend occasional mandatory meetings with the coven. She would grudgingly attend, grudgingly vote when a vote was called for. She spent no time on niceties and no time socializing.

As an interim leader of the coven—there'd been no leader since Mémé's mother had died—Michelina had attempted to bring Leandra into the coven, to get her to be a part of the group.

Leandra had no interest in it. She'd spent her time honing her witchcraft on her own, studying her grandmother's notes, practicing well into the midnight hours by candlelight.

Her days were spent searching out and healing injured swamp animals, evenings were dedicated to witchcraft, and her nights were haunted by a dark-haired, dark-eyed lion shifter who had made her body feel things she'd never felt before, without even a touch. Instead, he'd touched her soul, pulled her into a maelstrom that promised her things she'd never imagined existed.

Lucia had disappeared from Leandra's life after that lunch, and only an occasional postcard in the mailbox—no postmark—let Leandra know her aunt was still alive and keeping an eye on her.

Today's mail yielded yet one more postcard.

"Quake. Noon."

That was all the postcard read.

Block writing that resembled Lucia's.

Leandra dropped the card on the kitchen table.

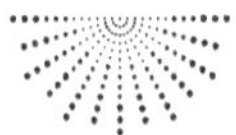

CHAPTER TEN

Quake
New Orleans, Louisiana

Theo slipped through the shifter door at Quake. He couldn't explain it, but there was something about Lucia that he trusted. It seemed completely natural to him that he come to Quake as she'd said.

The hostess let him in and led him to the room he'd sat in before, the day he'd first seen Leandra.

He didn't occupy the large table in the middle. Instead, he chose a chair at the two-seater corner table. He ordered the daily special without looking at the menu. He couldn't have cared less what he ordered. He didn't plan to eat.

He hadn't been there ten minutes when her scent drifted toward his nostrils and filled his lungs.

Leandra.

A drumming sound filled his head, bounced off his mind, reverberated throughout his body. It took him a second to process this phenomenon, it was so new to him.

In truth, he admitted to himself with chagrin, he wouldn't have been able to place the cause without his lion's whispered thoughts.

Her heartbeat.

The drumming that filled his body and took over his pulse was Leandra's heartbeat.

The magnificence of this occurrence awed him. Could Leandra feel this? Was it the same for her?

The tempo became stronger, and he knew that meant she was approaching.

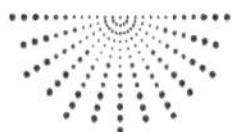

CHAPTER ELEVEN

Quake
New Orleans, Louisiana

Leandra followed the hostess down the hallway. She'd not given her a chance to ask for a table, or mention a section—nothing. She'd simply greeted Leandra with a swift smile, said she had her reservation ready and to follow her.

The hallway was dark red. Definitely the witches' section.

Of course, where else would they take me?

A weird sensation made her stumble. Leandra caught her fall against the hallway's wall.

It wasn't so much that she felt weak as there was this pounding in her head overtaking all her senses. She couldn't concentrate on anything else. It was like the bass from a teenager's car radio, reverberating throughout her body.

But there was no music.

There was nothing but the hostess, who glanced back and asked, "Are you okay?"

"You don't hear—feel—it?" Leandra fought the urge to cover her ears.

The sound grew louder and louder, eclipsing everything.

The hostess looked at her as if she'd lost it and took another step.

Leandra followed, but the sound and thumping intensified with every step.

She led her past the witches' section and into the first room in the shifter hallway.

"I— Wait I—" She couldn't find the words to ask the hostess why they weren't staying in the witches' area.

Maybe Lucia sat with her own kind today.

Leandra let the argument and questions building in her mind fade away. Lucia would explain when she sat down.

Except there was no Lucia.

There was only a wide-chested, broad-shouldered, dark-skinned man with a scowl on his face.

The throbbing in her head had become a drummer's solo.

"You." The whisper escaped her lips. She turned to the hostess, confused.

The hostess was gone.

"Leandra." He rose to his feet, a giant of a man compared to her height. His voice had a quality of a viscous liquid, covering her, insulating her from the world.

That's when she noticed it. The throbbing had subsided, turning into a syncopating beat that matched her heart.

She fought the urge to step closer to the man, to absorb his strength and make it her own. How would it be to be covered in his love, secure that nothing could penetrate their sphere?

"The beating…that was you?" she asked.

He shook his head. "That was us."

She studied the scowl on his face, wanted to smooth his forehead, send the thoughts that brought the frown away. "That's not possible."

"Possible?" He laughed, a grumbling sound that came from deep within his chest but didn't make the fierceness of his expression go away. "A witch says that something isn't possible?" He indicated the chair before her. "Joining me?"

"Why are you here?" She touched the chair's back, but, before she could move it, he'd pushed it aside and waited for her to sit. "Why am I here?"

"I have no way of knowing why you are here. I

was invited." His fingers brushed against her back as he settled her chair in place. The touch, brief as it was, scorched her flesh.

She noticed an accent—faint, foreign.

"Tell me about the raven-haired beauty sitting across from me," Theo said.

She felt an instant sunburn sensation on her cheeks. Why did his words bring a damned blush to her cheeks? She fought the urge to fan herself.

So much for asking about the accent.

She'd have to remember to ask him about it.

She looked into his eyes, drawn into their magnetic warmth. His lion flamed amber-and-gold specks in the depths.

And, as if he'd opened a floodgate in the world's leakiest, formerly strong dam, she burst.

And boy did she ever.

Hours passed, just the two of them. Hours and hours. Maybe an eternity.

"I tossed the skin bleach in the bayou." She wrapped up the bleach story.

He threw his magnificent head back, laughter rumbling and filling the room they still had to themselves.

Leandra flashed a smile. She could see herself with this man when he was a white-haired, old lion shifter.

She paused, surprised at the thought. But not at all put off by it.

"What's on your mind?"

"Nothing. Your turn. Tell me what I want to know about Theo Ricoletti."

"I don't know what you want to know." His teeth gleamed in the dimly lit room.

"I want to know everything about you. From start to finish."

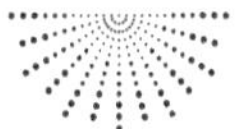

CHAPTER TWELVE

Quake
New Orleans, Louisiana

Theo's lion senses told him it was dark outside. He'd been in this room, with only this one woman, and it was as if they were the only beings in the universe. Their own universe.

They were in the midst of a spotlight in a darkened room, and nothing in the darkness seemed to matter to either of them.

She'd opened up and told him all about her mother's treatment of her. About her grandmother, the one she called Mémé, and the cabin in the swamp that she'd be happy to call home for the rest of her life.

It was his turn, and he found himself wanting to share for the first time in his life.

"My father took me from my mother. He then brought her to live nearby. He lost his first son, didn't really know him. A witch put a spell on Cristiano. The mother never told Marco about his son. The witch—his former lover—never told him about the spell. He found out about all this later. Too late for him and his son to have a relationship, I suppose. I'm not sure. All I know is Cristiano, his first son, doesn't keep up with him."

"Did you have a relationship with your father?"

"Not really. You can't kidnap a kid from his home, keep him from the only parent he's ever known for months without antagonizing the kid. I tried not to hate him. By the time my mother died, I'd have to say we had a friendship—not a close one though. And we never had a father-son relationship."

Never will.

"It's like you don't have family."

"Isn't that similar to your situation? It's like you don't either," he pointed out.

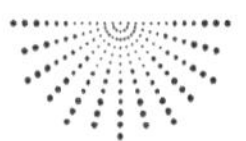

CHAPTER THIRTEEN

Quake
New Orleans, Louisiana

Leandra wished she could remember what they had for lunch. For the life of her, she couldn't. One minute she was sitting down at the table, joining this beautiful man, the next moment, her plate was half empty, his was completely clean, and they were standing up.

She'd never experienced anything like this before.

How could a man possibly affect her this way?

"Ready?" He pushed his chair away, rose to his feet, and helped her to hers.

Leandra followed him out of the dining room,

feeling much like a puppet being controlled by a puppeteer. "What did you do to me?"

They were in the vestibule that led to the front door, which would put them in the streets of New Orleans.

He stopped, turned around to face her. "I'm not sure what you mean."

"You don't do witchcraft." She scrutinized him. "Or do you?" It was as if she weren't the mistress of her own destiny or faculties.

His laughter was soft and rumbly. "Me, witchcraft? Not hardly." He stepped closer.

Having him so close made her breath catch in her throat. Leandra took a step back. "Theo." His name was a breathy whisper on her lips.

"Leandra." He leaned down, lowering his face to hers. She picked up the scent of pine woods and crisp cinnamon. His breath warmed her cheek. His eyes remained locked on hers.

Lower, and lower, and lower.

"It's nice to see you feel it, too."

"Why are you here?"

"Do not want me to be?" Warm air from his lips tickled the hair on her cheeks.

"You know what I mean. You didn't send for me. Someone else did. So how do you know? And why are you here? And why isn't she?"

"What makes you think I know anything? I was sent here."

He pressed her against the wall with his body, gently, yet with the strength of steel.

Every curve on her body yielded to the power in his.

The next moment, time stood still while he stared at her, lowering his head so slowly apprehension froze time.

He was so close she could smell the man of him, smell the lion of him, and imagined she could taste him. His nostrils flared, taking in her exhaled air, breathing it in deep, then letting the life-giving substance return to her, only to have her drink it in.

And yet his lips hadn't touched hers yet.

They alit gently, almost as if he was seeking sanction to touch her, approval to kiss her.

A button seemed to have been pushed within him. His lips immediately claimed hers, venturing in, declaring their possession. Diving in, his tongue was hot, challenging, greedy, demanding her acquiescence.

The galaxy began a fast rotation, taking both of them with it.

Nothing existed.

Nothing but Theo.

Breathless, she placed her hands on his chest. Leandra tried to push, she wanted to push him far

far away. But, at the same time, she wanted to pull him closer.

So, what did her treacherous hands do?

Her fingernails dug into his chest, that wide glorious musclebound chest of his. Betraying her, it almost looked like they were pulling him closer.

Theo pulled away, his eyes narrowing with desire. "Can you deny this?"

Leandra shook her head her, lower lip trembling.

"I'm coming to see you."

"You shouldn't."

"Tell that to my lion."

CHAPTER FOURTEEN

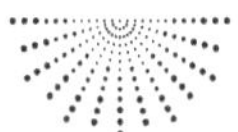

Black Glade Bayou, Louisiana

L eandra stared at the serpent. It stared back.

One of us is giving in. And it isn't me.

She pushed her thoughts toward the serpent.

Get thee from my grandmother's porch, else face my wrath.

The serpent slid its forked tongue out of a lipless mouth, flicked it her way.

Leandra blew a breath out slowly, letting it linger as the serpent tasted her scent.

The damned creature refused to yield its spot, raising its head threateningly.

Leandra's nostrils flared.

You had your chance.

She raised her right hand slightly, ready to send

the oversized dark, banded cottonmouth to its maker.

In the blink of an eye, less than a blink of an eye, an arrow pinned the snake's head to the porch's wooden column not far from Leandra's face.

"What the hell?" The whisper escaped her in a whoosh.

She glanced toward the wooded area just past the ramp that led to her grandmother's cottage.

She caught a glimpse of a shadow. Her eyes narrowed.

A large man stepped out from the undergrowth.

"Playing with snakes?" Theo's accented voice was thick with emotion.

She knew that emotion only too well. They'd become close in the last few months. He was a regular visitor at her cabin.

She never went to the Arceneaux property to see him. She knew Lézare Arceneaux's position on Theo being involved with a witch.

Particularly me.

She pushed away the sting of rejection. It stung even when the person delivering the rejection didn't matter.

"I'm not playing with snakes. He was trifling with me. And trespassing on my property. I warned him."

Theo laughed, the sound filling the swamp. Birds chirped in response. "You're living on the edge."

"A serpent cannot hurt me."

"Could a lion?"

"A lion could do anything he wanted. This lion could." She trailed a finger over his chest.

THEO FOUGHT his lion's urge to claim her mouth, her tongue, her heart. He wanted to rip every shred of clothing from Leandra's curvy body.

It was difficult not to take what he knew was his, what he was ready to claim. He lowered his lips, brushing them against hers, his tongue sliding, parting her lips, their breaths blending.

He stopped, pulling his lion back because he had almost thrust his tongue into her mouth and claimed hers. He wrapped his fingers in her twisted braids, twining, until his knuckles brushed her scalp, holding her tightly by her locks.

"I want you," he uttered into her mouth.

Her low moan shot adrenaline and desire through him, leaving him throbbing and yearning.

She slid her tongue along his lips. Leandra's arms wound upward, fingertips trailing along his arms, then along his shoulders, raking his skin, burrowing into his flesh.

Theo hoisted her, pushing her into the wall of her grandmother's porch, his lower body pinning hers. His hard-on pressing against the softness of her curves.

Her tongue teased his softly, as if asking for permission, as if she was still unsure.

His hand rose upward from her hip, over her waist, brushing the side of her breast, while his thumb slipped over the straining, pebbled peak, evident beneath the bra's flimsy fabric

"Theo." His name was a whisper on her lips.

It was the tone in her voice. Theo didn't catch it, but his lion did: the tiniest niggle of apprehension beneath the waves of desire.

He knew. Immediately.

She'd never been with a man before. This wild woman, roaming the swamp, dressed provocatively in something that could almost be called a cross between a sundress and a chemise, had never been with a man before.

Theo pulled back and ran a fingertip along her jawline. "Leandra."

Her eyes closed, slowly, the lightness eerie and sexy, pulling him into the vortex that promised him heaven.

Her chest rose and then a sigh followed, teasing his lips with her breath, teasing his heart with a promise.

"Trust me?"

"With my life," she uttered the words low.

He picked her up and carried her inside her grandmother's cabin.

In seconds, Theo had her stripped. She stood naked before him, a full-figured goddess, curved perfectly. He cupped her breasts, lifting the weight as if testing them, enjoying the way they overflowed his hand.

Her heartbeat raced, the pulse visible in her neck, then she groaned.

This threw Theo over the edge of self-control.

Fuck, he'd wanted their first time to be slow, but he couldn't. His lion wouldn't be contained. His lion had to have her now!

She pushed closer to him, as if telling him that she knew the need and was equally driven, and completely unafraid.

He brought his head down and took a hard nipple in his mouth. Her hands, already tangled in his head, pushed him lower while he sucked on a dusky tip.

He lowered his other hand, slowly, over a soft belly, then touched the top of her slit, careful not to encounter her clit.

Not yet.

"Theo," her low-spoken summons made his shaft jerk.

He let his finger slide along the slit, still careful not to touch her core of pleasure.

Heated moisture greeted his index finger as he lowered his hand, more and more. "So ready. For me." His words were a growl, powered by his yearning.

"Yessss," she hissed the word and leaned closer to him, her hips grinding her mound against his hand.

He thrust a finger in, unable to restrict the need to feel her heat surrounding him.

She gasped, took his finger in, her muscles tightening, her body pushing forward to take more.

He pulled it out, then pushed it in again, watching her face as desire crossed her features.

She writhed against him, her wetness dripping down his finger.

"I want to taste that sweetness."

"I want you. God, Theo. Now."

He studied her face, to be sure there was no fear, and found only her need for him there.

That was all it took to completely veer him off one course and onto another

She put her hands flat on his chest, running them lower. His stomach tightened as he held his breath. Bringing her close, trapping her eager fingers between their bodies, he drove his tongue into her mouth.

Head thrown back, her mouth yielded to him. He grabbed her in a fireman's carry and took her to the bed, his cock throbbing with every step as he drew closer to the mattress on the twin bed

God, please don't let me destroy that thing.

He knew it would be vigorous. The way he wanted her, it was bound to be.

A second later, they were on the bed, her leg wrapped around his waist. He pulled her leg away and lowered his head, her sweetness near his face. Theo inhaled, letting the scent of her sit on his senses, tempting his mouth, his tongue, his mind, cock, and fingers, too. Every part of her tempted him.

Desire to be with her, to be in her, to be a part of her was pulling at him with a force that defied all others. He slipped a hand beneath her, his finger slipping into her wet sheath. She moved and squirmed. The movement served to have her pushing his digit in even deeper.

He lowered his head even closer, letting her feel the warmth of his breath before he blew gentle cooling air on her heated moistness.

Theo wanted to rush it, to bury his face between her legs, to allow his tongue to replace his finger. He stared at the dusky lips that beckoned him with a lustrous wetness. The desire to replace his finger grew.

He watched her face as he pulled the finger out. Disappointment replaced lust, then he ran his finger upward toward a clit already engorged with need. Theo rubbed it softly, watching her eyes dilate with hunger, her hips arched, a groan filling the cabin's stillness.

His breath still hot on her sleek pussy, as he teased her little core.

Leandra's breasts heaved with every breath. Taut nipples pushed up, growing harder and harder.

Her body was an untouched banquet. Lush and made for passion—with him. Only him. And no man before him.

Or after me.

He wanted no other, and he knew she felt the same.

He raised one hand to her mound and stroked the nearest nipple while making tight circles on her clit with his thumb.

He delivered rapid flicks on her clit while her hips rose and writhed.

Her sweet puckered folds were covered in moistness.

While his thumb took care of her clit, his middle finger slid closer toward her hot sheath, playing near the entrance. He twirled it, loving the sounds of her wetness merging with her light moans.

Theo lowered his head, giving it a tiny lick, then taking a long slow deliberate swipe at her folds, lapping her flavor in.

She panted then released a long moan.

His cock strained, wanting her, pushing against the bed, seeking the warmth of her, though Theo denied himself the pleasure.

He'd wait.

In Theo's mind, his lion bellowed frustration at the denial of an immediate mating.

Theo ate her sweetness with a reckless and uncontrolled appetite. He spread her lips farther to get at the sleekness inside, sucking on her lips, pushing his tongue in and out.

He pressed his tongue deeper, burying his face in, relishing the taste, the scent, the texture.

Fuck. She was amazing.

He groaned with a desire that was being denied while she bucked against his mouth. Lips buried into her folds, he sucked her sensitive bud in, flicking it with his tongue. Delivering a volley of tongue flicks that left her a trembling, creamy muddle, her hands buried in his head, her nails digging in, drawing blood.

She arched her hips and rose, almost to a sitting position as she released, while he licked the creamy results of her passion.

His lion and Theo had taken all they could.

He let his lion take over as he thrust into her, reveling at her cry when he'd filled her and stretched her to accommodate him.

"God, I'm sorry baby. I didn't mean to hurt you." He drew away.

She grabbed his hips and pulled him in closer, ramming him deep inside.

Theo drove in deep, and pulled back, then deep again, while she squirmed and clawed at his back, scoring his flesh with a searing pain that merged with the pleasure.

"Beautiful," he groaned against her mouth. "Fucking amazing." He slammed into her with a fervor that heralded a need he'd never before felt.

Leandra met his every drive with a hunger that matched his.

He pulled her in close for a kiss, while his other hand sought her clit, teasing circles on the swollen nub.

Her eyes flew open, and her lips parted, preparing to scream. He locked onto her mouth and swallowed her scream in deep, as she clenched around him repeatedly in orgasm.

The sound of her passion, muffled by his mouth was his undoing.

Her body pushed him closer to the edge. He groaned, and with a grunt and an uncontrolled rush, he came undone, holding her close.

Her curves collapsed against him.

All mine.

"I'm leaving the country for a week. Promise not to replace me with any random shifters? Or serpents?" Theo gave her a smile.

"Never."

And she meant it. She had the man she wanted. If only they could have each other fully without sneaking around, hiding from his boss and her coven.

CHAPTER FIFTEEN

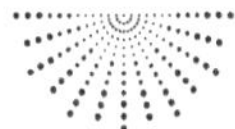

Black Glade Bayou, Louisiana

Leandra shifted in her seat. Clothing and shoes instead of barefoot in her usual practically threadbare chemise. A formal meeting at the Black Glade Coven Hall, that was the occasion behind Leandra's dressing up.

Her lips curved into a smile from the early morning's visit from Theo. Two months. She'd seen Theo Ricoletti regularly every few days now of the last two months. His visits were the one thing she had to look forward to in her life. She couldn't keep the pace of hiding him from others forever. Their relationship would be known quickly at this pace.

Michelina, the interim leader, rose to her feet.

"Council needs to find a new leader. We've gone long enough without one."

"We've managed fine so far. What's the rush?" Leandra asked.

"Adelise put the matter on the agenda."

"Of course she did." Leandra barely controlled the sneer that threatened to mar her features. She turned a tight smile toward Adelise and her sisters, all sitting at the table catty-corner to her own.

What a time to be sitting alone at a table. It really hit home, times like these, that her Mémé was gone. That Lucia wasn't around. And as for Rochelle—Leandra couldn't bring herself to call her mother, Rochelle had never sat at this table, to Leandra's knowledge.

She tried to focus on what the other witches were discussing.

"Technically, the leadership position would belong to a Mathieu," declared Councilmember Michelina. "But things have changed. Latrice chose to have a shifter's child, making herself unable to be leader. Rochelle has spurned the coven. Lucia is the offspring of a shifter, so automatically not qualified to lead witches." Michelina turned accusing eyes toward Leandra. "And you…" She shook her head, as if in disbelief.

Or maybe it's disappointment, Leandra pondered.

Michelina's eyes glowed in the dim room as she

continued. "You have chosen to cavort with shifters. Specifically, a lion shifter. Or so word has it."

The smirk on Adelise's face told Leandra exactly who had told the council this information.

Mémé had always said she'd wanted the leadership back in their family's control. Leandra had wanted to make her grandmother's dream come true —but was it really Mémé's dream? She had given up the dream willingly herself, to have the child of Étienne.

Maybe it wasn't Leandra's responsibility. But at the same time, it galled her to think Adelise's family would be able to take control of the coven her grandmother's grandmother once led.

A commotion at the doorway drew all eyes in the room.

She turned to see what the fuss was.

Rochelle walked in.

Except this wasn't the mother she remembered. The mother she hadn't seen in more than a decade.

Rochelle was different.

The room released a collective gasp.

"Rochelle." Michelina stood, her black gown majestic as it draped her body.

Leandra glanced between the woman who'd birthed her, and Michelina, who'd been responsible for some of Leandra's early training.

Rochelle was resplendent in a crimson dress so

dark it glowed like a glass of merlot in front of a candle. Her skin, always so pale, compared to Leandra's, glowed a ghostly white.

Leandra didn't need an explanation. She knew why the room gasped, and she knew why Rochelle's skin was so fair. When Rochelle's fevered black-and-crimson eyes rested on Leandra, the difference in her mother was apparent.

She'd been turned.

Rochelle Mathieu had become a vampire.

Her mother was now a vampire.

The enemy.

Rochelle's gaze was more like a glare as she stared at the daughter she'd scorned and rejected. Then she turned her eerie stare and focused on the council. "Michelina." A small scoff escaped from perfectly glossed lips. She shifted her weight slightly, from one foot to the other, turning her attention to Adelise. "You think yours can take away what belongs to my family?"

"Since when am I your family?" The whispered words escaped Leandra's lips before her brain could clamp her mouth shut. Leandra squeezed her hands into fists, pressed them into her thighs, pushing against her own flesh, wishing she were anywhere but here. Anywhere at all.

Rochelle swiveled toward Leandra slowly, with

deliberate moves. One perfectly arched brow rose. Disdain crossed her features. She shook her head.

I see I still disappoint you. Leandra thanked the stars she managed to think it and not say it.

Could a vampire hurt her? She'd faced vampires before. She could kill a vampire.

But could I kill a vampire that's also my mother?

Rochelle left the room. Behind her, the witches' conversations were a loud buzzing sound in Leandra's mind. She couldn't pick one conversation apart from another one.

So much buzzing going on.

A gavel pounding on wood brought the room to a silence.

"Enough theatrics and distractions. We have a purpose for today's meeting, vampires aside. We've been hired to protect a shifter—one Alexandria Arceneaux."

"Since when do shifters hire us to protect them?" Leandra asked.

"Since we can provide a service, and they have something we want."

"Pray tell what that is." Leandra tried but couldn't remember ever seeing this Alexandria.

"Territory. Without a fight. No battle. No bloodshed."

Since when does a witch run from a confrontation.

Surely, they could take this territory by force.

Michelina raised her hand, as if anticipating Leandra's objections. "A majority vote has been taken. The coven is in agreement. All that's left to decide is who is going to do the deed."

"The deed?" Leandra asked.

"The lion shifter security guard must protect the Arceneaux woman. A spell, to have him fall in love with her, guarding her, with his life, this must be done."

Leandra fought back the gasp. She couldn't allow this to happen. She couldn't have another witch handling this, making him fall in love with the Arceneaux shifter woman forever. There was only one option. Especially if she didn't want to lose Theo.

"I'll do it."

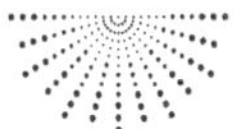

CHAPTER SIXTEEN

Black Glade Bayou, Louisiana

Leandra kneeled and studied the track. Definitely a large feline, but not as large as Theo's lion's tracks were.

And it was fresh.

Could it be?

"Lucia. Come out."

Lucia stepped out from between the overgrown cypress trees.

"You are good," her aunt said.

"To what do I owe the pleasure of your company?" Leandra studied her aunt, wondering why she'd come, why she didn't send a postcard, and why she'd stayed away since that last postcard, the one that had her join Theo.

"You must do this. It is written. If you do not do what is fated, if you try to avert…the shifter will not live."

How does she know what I've agreed to do?

"What do you mean, exactly."

"There's no reason to pretend I don't know what you've agreed to, Leandra. And I know why. Everything is as it should be, but I wanted to be sure you had no hesitations."

"But I do have hesitations. Lots of them. He's the man I— He's— Theo is…" Leandra sucked the bayou's air in but couldn't get enough to make her struggling lungs happy.

Or maybe it wasn't her lungs that weren't working so much as it was that her heart was struggling not to break.

"Lucia." Leandra closed her eyes briefly to compose herself, then opened them again. "The spell I'm to put on him… What if I don't do it correctly? What if he falls in love with this Alexandria? What if they bond?" Her heart tightened, squeezing with a ferocity that brought tears to her eyes.

"I will help you put it together."

"You? But you are not a practicing witch."

"That doesn't mean I wasn't trained in the craft of our family." Lucia gave her a nod. "Let's go. We have work to do. Your man will be back tonight, won't he? From his trip?"

A shiver crossed over Leandra. How did her aunt know so much? "He returns tonight."

"And as usual, you will be the first thing on his mind."

Leandra couldn't help the smile that crept to her face. She knew Theo made seeing her a priority.

"How long must I keep the farce up?"

"You will know. Trust your visions."

"What if it's a dream? Wishful thinking while I lay in a half-asleep state?"

"You will have to discern and be honest with yourself. You know the price."

"You never visit during times of joy, do you?"

Sadness passed over Lucia's face. "Seems that is my role, these days."

"Who do you answer to? Where do you get all this information?"

Lucia shook her head. "It's not for me to tell. Maybe it never will be." She rolled up her sleeves. "Let's get to work."

THEO'S PULSE raced with excitement. He hadn't seen her in a few days, but it felt like it had been an eternity. He made his way through the undergrowth, ignoring the scratches from thorns and errant branches.

On stilts that were watermarked—depicting how high the water had risen at various times, and proving the stilts were needed—Leandra's grandmother's cabin was an unpainted, weathered wooden structure, not much bigger on the outside than the cabins at Arceneaux Point. Entrenched tightly amongst the rot-resistant cypress trees, the building looked as if it had been there for ages, the roots and branches of the trees had begun to grow around the cabin's frame, making it appear as if it were an organic, nature-created creation. From the roof of the cabin, a ladder, part wood, part rope, rose and rose and became lost amongst the tall trees in the swamp.

Mist surrounded the ramp that connected the slight cabin's wraparound dilapidated porch. The entrance of the ramp was half-buried on solid ground, then it extended over the water, eventually touching the porch.

Leandra stood in the doorway of her grandmother's cabin, the light behind her casting her body in a tempting silhouette.

She was clad in one of the threadbare chemises she wore when she was at home, alone, in the bayou.

The way the fabric clung to her curves, the way the material was diaphanous in just the right light. It was far more magnificent than anything else he could imagine her wearing.

She was regal.

She was royalty.

She was Theo's first and only love.

She was his.

Theo would die rather than be with another.

His lion roared in agreement.

Theo's strides became longer, faster as he hastened his way up the ramp to meet the love of his life.

His lips closed in, swooping down like a bird of prey. His mouth crashed into hers, and his tongue drove in, branding and claiming.

Leandra returned the kiss, and he could see that her own passion was fueled by his.

She pulled away, held him at arms' length and studied his face as if trying to memorize his features. A glimmer of melancholy shone in her eyes briefly.

The scent of her—a heady fragrance, sweet, with a hint of the herbs she kept in the cabin—filled his lungs, teasing his appetite with a suggestion of her flavor. He dropped into a gulf of yearning. The sensation rolled over him in waves.

This woman was his.

Had always been meant to be his.

He reached for her chemise and pulled it over her head. She stood before him, legs shoulder-width apart, hands on her hips, a curvaceous goddess, splendid in the setting sun. Her white bra showcased her breasts, so full they were overflowing the cups.

Her white cotton panties clung to her mound, teasing him with the outline of the treasure within.

"Lose the bra." His voice was husky, his lion making the request, though it sounded more like an order.

A quick reach and snap of two fingers, and the cotton hung loose, cups clinging to the bounty within.

Theo pulled it off, relished the sight of her. Her breasts, a lighter café au lait were garnished with dusky rose tips.

Screw the panties. He released one of his claws and drew it across the fabric on both hips.

The panties fell to the wood floor of the threshold with a silent whisper.

He cupped her breasts, thumbs brushing over taut pearlized nubs. Theo pinched a nipple and Leandra gasped in response. He lowered his head, touched his tongue to the tip. His thumb caressed the other nipple, rolling over it, pressing it in, then pulling on it, pinching it.

Leandra's gaze was fixed on him, pupils dilated. Her scent rose, growing stronger.

His lion growled in response, his cock twitched.

Theo lowered his hand, wandering over her stomach while his tongue toyed with her nipple and he alternately sucked and flicked, then grazed it with his teeth as his hand passed over her thigh and made for the moist target in the middle.

Her heartbeat thudded in his mind, trying to match his. He slid a finger over her sensitive little core and she flinched, almost jumping.

He parted her folds with his fingers, enjoying the scent that rose. He glided a finger along her wet folds, near the heat of her entrance.

A moan escaped Leandra. She spread her legs farther.

The scent of her became sheer torture. Her nails dug into his shoulders as he lowered himself, eye level to her pussy, where a nicely trimmed triangle of dark hair greeted him.

Theo paused to breathe her in, letting her essence sit on his palate, teasing himself with the taste of her scent.

One thumb on her clit, the other hand parting her, he blew on her mound, a slight breeze cooling her heated flesh.

His cock throbbed with need, demanding access. He led her to the kitchen chair facing the door and sat her down.

Her eyes grew wide. "What if someone approaches?"

"I'll hear them." Not that she ever had visitors out

here. He'd never seen a soul. He spread her legs and leaned back, admiring. "God, I've missed you."

Her eerie, sexy eyes glowed luminescent in the near darkness in the unlit room.

Theo leaned in, his breath hot on her mound. Hotter than the Louisiana bayou environment.

He swiped at her with his tongue, from the top of her entrance down over her clit.

She twitched in response.

That was the moment he drove two fingers in, stretching her while she was in the middle of flexing. She wiggled and slanted her body forward, wanting more.

He licked her clit, his tongue flicking with super-natural speed while his fingers pumped in and out, over and over.

"*Sacre bleu*," she panted.

He picked up speed, relentless in his quest for her pleasure. "Come for me, now." His demand was a growl, low, heated.

She put her legs on his shoulders, locking his head between them, while her muscles tightened around his fingers.

Leandra screamed his name as climax after climax overtook her.

A glistening moisture on her face made him think he'd seen a tear. He studied her countenance.

Theo tipped her chin upward. "Are you crying?"

"Tears of joy." Her lips curved into a smile that was almost bittersweet then she licked his bottom lip.

She pulled him close, rocked her hips, and pressed him against her moisture then guided his length inside her.

LEANDRA FOUGHT BACK the thoughts that this would be the last time for a long time she made love to Theo. She didn't yield to the idea that if things went wrong, this would be the last time ever. That he'd forever forget what they were to one another.

"I love you," she whispered in his ear, her words accentuated by the crickets and frogs outside the cabin.

She wrapped her arms around his neck and hoisted herself closer to him, taking him in as deep as she could.

"I love you, too. Forever," he groaned.

He began to pump, pulling, then pushing, deeper and deeper, making her gasp with every thrust.

Theo watched his cock going into her, taking her, possessing her. And Leandra watched his face, savoring and memorizing the look of passion merged with love.

She squeezed, tightening around him, making

him growl. He leaned forward, locked her lips with his. She could taste herself on his lips.

Leandra dug her nails into the flesh of his neck, making him grunt with the pleasure and pain, while at the same time driving her to greater heights. His large hands dug into her hips and ass, raising her and pulling her closer, driving into her, deep, hard, pushing, demanding.

She buried her head into his chest so he wouldn't see the tears that were free-flowing, while she tried to regain her composure.

"Forgive me, my love," she whispered the words against his chest. "It's the only way. It won't be forever."

I hope.

THEO SHOOK his head in confusion. Where the hell was he? He looked around the dilapidated little abode, the tiny bed he'd just gotten out of.

He was nude, in front of a—

—the swamp witch!

He pulled away from her. Her hands had been on his chest.

"What the hell am I doing here? How'd I—"

Fuck. He'd been having sex with her?

What the hell is wrong with me?

Why was he here? He shouldn't be talking to an Arceneaux enemy, much less sleeping with one.

He studied the dark-skinned beauty before him.

Tears glistened on her cheeks.

Why was she crying? He hadn't... Had he?

He shook his head once more while deep within, his lion roared.

He sought his clothing, found it on the floor, and was out the door, fastening buttons as he ran down the ramp that led to the swamp.

I don't know what the hell just happened, but I'm not telling Lézare a thing until I figure out what's going on.

APART AND TOGETHER AGAIN

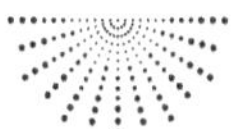

Months and More Months Passed

And so it was, for months and months, then months turning into years, Leandra tethered the spell that bound Theo into loving Alexa Arceneaux. Loving Alex just enough to protect her, but not enough to push them into a bonding. That Leandra couldn't do. She couldn't face the idea of losing the only man she'd ever wanted. The only man she ever would want.

The only one for her.

She kept an eye from afar, carefully controlling the spell that kept Alexa and Theo bound, not allowing it to become that which Leandra's heart feared most.

~

LEANDRA KEPT TO HERSELF, avoided coven politics, studied the craft her grandmother had loved so much, and grew her powers. She'd tested her strength against the occasional vampire that crossed paths with her, and was victorious.

Leandra had arrived to a state of sorcery where, unbeknownst to her and to many of the Black Glade Coven, she'd become the most powerful witch in the area.

This meant nothing to the cappuccino-tinted, dark-haired beauty that no longer smiled.

And then one day, unexpectedly, she received the sign her heart had been waiting for. She prayed it wasn't too late.

Leandra had a vision of Alexa and a wolf. Leandra traveled onto forbidden Arceneaux territory, visiting the former plantation cabins at Arceneaux Point where she met the wolf from her vision.

Alexa's wolf.

Reese.

Alexa's fated mate.

This was during the Escape Weekend which held the Shifter Masquerade Ball and other shifter events.

Leandra became an accessory in the Arceneaux sisters' adventures without the knowledge of their big brother Lézare.

And it wasn't long, before she'd joined in on their escapades, saving the life of more than one Arceneaux.

Leandra wondered if, somewhere from witch heaven, her Mémé wasn't smiling.

Unless she's turning over in her grave at the idea that I'm helping the Arceneaux.

ALEXA ARCENEAUX STOOD before Leandra in Mémé's cabin.

"Changes are coming to Arceneaux Point." Leandra felt odd repeating the words from her dream.

Alexa's eyes narrowed. "What?"

Leandra felt him. There was no way Theo could sneak up on her at this stage. She was too connected to him. And as silently and stealthily as he tried to move up the ramp, she sensed him, felt his heartbeat with her own.

The door flew open.

"Alexa! What the hell are you thinking? Your brother has forbidden you from coming here alone." Theo barely gave Leandra a glance.

The sting of seeing him so close and not having him, of not being his woman made her nose burn with unshed tears.

"Theo! Why are you skulking through the bayou following me?" Alexa's face reddened in anger.

Leandra didn't breathe a sigh of relief out loud, but was happy Alexa hadn't formed an attraction for Leandra's man.

Theo squared his shoulders. "Lézare told me to watch you while he was out of town. Seems he knows your propensity for trouble."

"Theo Ricoletti." Leandra unfolded legs tucked beneath her as she perched on the banister and rose from her seat.

"Witch," he scoffed.

That stings.

Alexa looked between the two of them, curiosity on her face.

I wonder if she can sense our chemistry.

"Lézare shouldn't have felt the need to have you protect his sister from me." Leandra crossed her arms over her chest, using arrogance to mask her pain and the love she felt for Theo. "Me, of all people. As if I'd do an Arceneaux harm."

Theo didn't respond. He put a hand on Alexa's arm. "Let's go."

Alexa yanked herself from his grasp. "I'm not going until I've talked to Leandra."

Oh, no. This could get ugly.

Theo's eyes narrowed, his nostrils flared. A growl came from deep within his chest. His dark-brown eyes flared with an amber light. "Then I go with you." He took a step onto the ramp, which sunk into the soft dirt with his wide shouldered, thick chested bulk.

Alexa glared at his back.

Leandra shook her head, tried to keep from appraising his body—the body that had brought her so much joy. "He is no different than he was years ago, on a rampage, angry at the world, this lion shifter." She forced amusement into her tone.

The growl in Theo's chest became louder.

Alexa followed him up the ramp.

Leandra opened the door to her cabin and entered, Theo and Alexa followed behind.

Leandra sat then nodded toward the chair across from her. "Sit."

Alexa looked at Theo, then back at Leandra.

"Be seated," Leandra repeated.

Alexa joined her at the table while Theo leaned against the doorjamb.

"I'm fine right here, thank you for the hospitality, Miss Mathieu." A fake smile remained on his face, pulling his features tight.

Leandra nodded, but her heart was pierced by his formality.

"What changes are coming to Arceneaux Point?" Alexa jumped right in.

"I can only tell you the essence of matters."

Theo released a soft snort. "Basically, nothing." He rubbed his nose as if offended. "Witchery."

Leandra bristled.

"You are welcome to leave, Theodoros Ricoletti, son of an Italian lion shifter and his Greek servant woman, raised by the servants in secret until the lion shifter learned he had a son. Theodoros Ricoletti, stolen by his lion shifter father from his servant woman mother, reared by governesses and nannies."

Theo flinched. His eyes narrowed, muscles flexed in arms clad in a short sleeve shirt.

"Does my recounting of your life need any correction, lion? Would you like me to provide more of your history?" The flame of anger at their situation lit her cheeks on fire.

"You've said enough, witch."

"Why does Theo hate you?" Alexa asked.

"He knew me before…" Leandra glanced at the bed, then away quickly, making her face an unreadable mask.

"What is the essence of what you feel? What sort of changes at Arceneaux?" Alexa persisted.

"You know Lézare would not be happy with this." Theo's words were clipped, coming from a clenched jaw.

Leandra had heard enough of Lézare. A day of reckoning with that man would come. "He would be happy if he knew my efforts could save lives. You send Lézare to me, if need be."

"Would you two quit bickering?" Alexa slapped the tabletop, making it reverberate. "Save lives? What changes are coming to Arceneaux Point?"

"New mates, new types of beings. Some friendly, some not so much." Pushing away from the table, Leandra rose from her chair.

"That's it? How am I supposed to…? What am I to do with this information?"

"Be accepting. Be forgiving. Be vigilant. And be happy."

Theo released a scoffing laugh. "That's all you have, witch?" He took a step toward Leandra.

Leandra backed up. She had no idea how she would handle it if the man she loved tried to hurt her. She'd have to use her witchcraft to protect herself.

Luckily, Alexa rose to intercept him.

He froze, his gaze a squint, a flash of amber in his eyes.

"What's this?" Theo reached for an object on a shelf.

Leandra gasped. How the hell did he see it?

"Leave it." Leandra snatched the object from him, ran toward the door, and, before Alexa could react, she'd said a few words and tossed it out.

It splashed when it hit the water and sank immediately.

"What were you doing, witch?" Theo wrapped a large hand around her wrist. "What have you been up to?"

"Theo, don't hurt her." Alexa put her hand on his arm.

His head snapped in Alexa's direction. His dark eyes had become fully amber, heralding an impending shift. He dropped on all fours. Theo's face widened, then a tawny muzzle began to take form, thick wiry whiskers poked through the skin on his face.

Bones crunched, tendons tore, creaking presaged his change into a large, dark-maned lion.

Leandra raised her arms. She'd have to protect herself. Maybe even Alexa.

Alexa's eyes closed, then they flew open. Sinew and muscles lengthened painfully, flesh stretched, fur emerged. A growl emanated from her widening chest.

In her tigress form, Alexa stood to her full height in front of the large lion that Theo had become.

His lion rumbled at Alexa.

Alexa's tigress snarled back.

He leaned back and opened his cavernous mouth wide, jaws spread, teeth bared and gleaming. He released a roar that shook the cabin's contents, leaving tiny glass goblets tinkling as they clinked into each other.

Leandra hadn't told Theo that she could listen in and join shifters in the syncs—their silent means of communication when in their shifted form. The way the shifters minds linked up to talk.

Leandra felt Theo push Alexa for a link.

She felt Alexa accept his request, and then Leandra silently joined them, eavesdropping.

"Leave," Theo commanded Alexa.

"I'm not going. You can't hurt her."

Alexa was protecting her? Leandra began to like this Arceneaux woman even more.

"My lion wants to—" Theo pawed at the pine floor. His claws extending, blade-sharp, they dug into the wood, dragged across, leaving deep cream-colored gashes in the weathered dark flooring.

Leandra wondered what his lion wanted. She felt his pulse racing, driving hers to rise.

"Shift back, please. Let's talk this out," Alexa said.

"No!" Theo released another roar, this time in the sync.

Leandra fought the urge to cover her ears. She didn't want to divulge she was eavesdropping, though she did need to tell Theo as soon as possible.

"Shift. I'm asking you as your boss's sister."

Leandra took a gamble. Surely their love could overcome this. "I know you won't hurt me. I know you can't. You, the one I couldn't control. You're not as easy as Theo, are you, *chère*?"

Seconds later, after more creaking and stretching, then contracting, Alexa shifted into her human form, then staggered, starting to fall.

Leandra leapt forward and caught her before she could dive headfirst into a bookshelf that housed glass, ceramic, and porcelain pestles, bowls, and cups.

Alexa held on to Leandra for support.

"I've got you, Alexa," Leandra whispered, then turned to Theo's lion. "Bring Theo back, brave lion. I promise, no spells."

The lion released a chuffing sound.

He stretched, his jaws opened in what looked like a yawn. Within seconds, his muscles contracted and his body morphed, bringing Theo back and pushing the lion into the man she loved once more.

Theo glanced at Alexa, then his stare pinned Leandra. His face turned ashen under his olive complexion. He shook his head as if confused.

Leandra stared at him defiantly. "I did what I had to do to protect Alexa."

To save us.

How could she even begin to explain this? She would. As soon as the dust settled.

Still shaking his head, he paused, then asked, "What is going on? Why do I…?" He rubbed his face, then ran his fingers over his head. "Leandra?" He put his arms out.

Leandra leaned into his embrace. Her heartrate matching his "I'm here. I'm sorry."

"Why do I remember? Why didn't I before?"

"Your blood. It was in the vial I tossed out."

"You collected my blood?"

"Not I. But it was given to me and, with it, an ultimatum. I did it to protect you. To protect her." She indicated Alexa.

"So why did you throw it away? Why now, after all this time?"

She cast her eyes down. When she raised her head, she couldn't see through unshed tears. "It was in a vision. These things must play out, though I do not always understand them." She was rambling, unsure what she was saying.

His lips alit on Leandra's forehead, then he pulled back. "You cast a spell on me? You made me forget about us? And made me think I was in love with Alexa?" His thumb traced her lower lip.

Alexa stared at them silently. To Leandra, she was barely there.

"I had to, my love. It was that or…" More tears sprang to Leandra's eyes. "I had to. You'd have been killed if anything were to happen to Alexa."

He frowned. "So you made me love her?" He held Leandra at arm's length. "When you knew all I wanted was you?" His voice was raw, the questions wrenched from his soul.

"Alexa had to be protected, and this was decided."

"And you agreed." Theo let the words fall with a finality.

Leandra was crestfallen. "If anyone else had put the spell on you, they'd have made it too powerful. I had to make your feelings for her just strong enough to love her a little. I couldn't have you taking her for a mate. I couldn't watch my man become another woman's. This can't come out," Leandra beseeched Theo.

"I'm not living a farce anymore." He turned toward Alexa. "I'm not trying to be cruel I don't want to hurt you… I'm sorry…"

"Theo." Leandra indicated Alexa. "Alexa has to be protected until she's mated. That's the decision."

"What?" His lion's grumble sounded in his chest.

"Just a while longer." Leandra worried her bottom lip with her teeth. "Alexa's time to find a mate is near. We keep this going for a few short days." Leandra explained to them what she could, though some of the mystery remained for her. The coven had made a deal with the shifters. Land in exchange for Alexa's protection.

Alexa and Theo nodded.

He leaned close. "I will come to see you as soon as possible." Theo took Leandra in his arms.

"Soon," Leandra whispered.

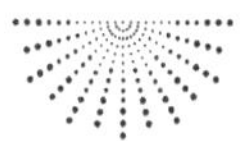

CHAPTER SEVENTEEN

A few short days later, just as the vision had foreshadowed, Alexa was mated to the wolf shifter Reese and Theo was free.

Almost free.

With a still lukewarm—more like ice cold—reception from Lézare, Leandra and Theo traveled together to New Orleans to help the Arceneaux shifters with an underground fighting ring that was costing local shifters their lives.

Leandra's assistance in diagnosing a shifter with Brahnson's Touch, an infliction that made shifters dangerously strong while at the same time deteriorating their brain matter so that right and wrong became twisted, and base needs were paramount.

Leandra was instrumental in the effort to save

Lézare Arceneaux's youngest sister from the fighting ring.

Theo felt this was the time to make things right between the Mathieu and the Arceneaux, though he had no idea if it were possible because he still didn't know the cause of the rift.

Except that shifters and witches are enemies.

But Lézare's animosity seemed personal.

Theo's last nerve had been assaulted when Lézare had called her a swamp witch while she'd been assisting to save Evie. He'd snapped, calling his best friend and boss out.

Lézare hadn't said much, but he'd appeared taken aback.

Now, the rescue effort was over and it was time to go home. Theo stood back from the group. His arm around Leandra. He'd never envisioned a life away from Arceneaux, they were like family to him now, but where the Arceneaux were his family, Leandra was his universe.

Lézare stepped forward. "We should get back to Arceneaux Point," he announced. "We need to make arrangements." Then he turned to Leandra. "Would you be our guest and stay at Arceneaux Point?"

Theo's mouth damned near dropped in surprise. He glanced at Leandra.

Her eyes gleamed silver. "Could I stay in one of the cabins?"

"Certainly." Lézare smiled, though apprehension lurked in his eyes. He nodded at Theo. The hatchet had been buried.

Theo released a soft breath of relief. New beginnings perhaps.

For all of us.

EPILOGUE

Leandra knelt onto the ground. Theo was at Arceneaux Point, working strategy with Lézare, and she'd slipped out of their cabin at Arceneaux Point to visit Mémé's cabin.

She and Theo had been together for more than two months now. She hadn't told him, though she wondered if his shifter senses had picked it up. She didn't plan to keep it a secret, but she wanted to be sure there'd be no complications. The worst thing that could have happened would be to have his hopes rise and then to have them dashed if she had a miscarriage.

Few shifter/witch babies made it past the first trimester. If they could get past those first few months, then they'd be out of the danger zone.

She should have noticed her surroundings. She

should have noticed the sun was going down. She should have noticed the wildlife's lullabies—crickets, birds, frogs—had stopped.

But she didn't. She was so focused on the herbs she knew would be growing out here.

"Look. Look what we have here."

Her head snapped in the direction of the voice while a shiver coursed through her body.

"No," the whisper escaped her lips. This couldn't be.

Four vampires, fangs gleaming behind smiles designed to frighten.

"She's a witch," a younger vampire said, blond hair buzz cut, muscles pushing out his T-shirt. There was fear in his voice.

For that, Leandra was happy. She needed them to fear her. She didn't want them to know her vulnerabilities.

To the side, another vampire laughed. He was older, regal, and his face had no shadow of fear on it. "She's harmless." He laughed once more, the sound filling the swampy bayou clearing. "She's more than harmless. Aren't you, swamp witch?"

The three younger vampires took a step closer to Leandra. Then another.

Leandra remained silent. She couldn't tell them. She wouldn't tell them. She rose to her feet slowly, stood at her full stature, which wasn't much—it was not like she was tall. Leandra did her best to look down her nose at them.

Sure, she could kill a vampire, quicker than a snap of her fingers. But not four. Not quickly enough.

All it took was one. If one vampire could get past her spell, if one vampire could strike her with his fangs, the contamination would kill the child growing within her.

Theo's child. Theo's daughter.

She wouldn't have that.

She'd die before the baby came to harm.

"There's only one way to know." She kept her voice even and pointed at the older vampire. "You're first, since you seem to think you know me." She gave him the smile she knew spelled death.

The other vampires backed up a pace.

The old vampire paled further beneath his already deathly white skin. "You can't touch me, witch. Your baby will be dead before you can raise your arms."

"Do you realize it's almost dark?" Theo stepped out of the shadows.

"Theo," she gasped his name. "You must leave. Now." Her lion shifter mate was no match for the vampires. No shifter was. Maybe Valencia Arceneaux, the hybrid vampire shifter, was, but Theo was no hybrid. "Leave. Please."

Theo laughed. He almost doubled over in laughter.

That moment, more than any other, more than anything, she knew the power of her man's love.

He laughed at the face of death.

Tears formed in her eyes. She'd not live without him and his daughter.

"You must go," she begged.

The old vampire joined in Theo's mirth. "The dead shifter is laughing, and he doesn't even know he's already dead." His eyes glowed crimson, his white hair, immaculately coiffed, was pushed back from his face.

A snarl, deep within Theo's chest rumbled, making her tremble.

"You think I travel alone?" Theo's voice was almost a lion's growl.

Leandra did a double take. What did that mean? Had he brought his security team with him? That would be a bloodbath, but maybe—just maybe—if he brought enough of them, then they'd stand a chance.

If only they can make a circle around me. I can work some magic, keep the baby safe from vampire blood, and— yes, just maybe they'd stand a chance.

Except, only one shifter stepped out of the shadows.

Lucia.

We are so in trouble.

Lucia's gaze fell on Leandra. "Niece. You look well, considering."

As if mirroring Leandra's thoughts, the old vampire began to laugh once more. "I was so hoping we'd have an even competition. This hardly seems fair."

Theo had a look of confusion on his face. "Considering? What's that mean?"

"He doesn't know?" Lucia frowned at Leandra.

Leandra fought the urge to groan. "Is this really the time? We're vampire appetizers."

"Yeah, we're going to make time." Theo's tone was resolute. "What do I not know?"

And with that, the old vampire's laughter became hysterical. His companion vampires joined in.

"She's carrying a baby. Surely, you know what happens when an unborn shifter baby is touched by vampire blood?"

Leandra fumed. "You mean contaminated."

"Semantics," the old vampire smirked. "Same outcome. Lights out, shifter baby. Permanently."

Theo glanced from Leandra to the vampire then back to Leandra again. "Is this true? Why don't I know?"

"I wanted to be sure she—the baby—was out of the danger zone."

"I have a daughter?"

"Had." The old vampire straightened the lapel on

the dark suit he was wearing. "Had, because"—he pulled an old-fashioned timepiece from a little pocket on his vest—"within fifteen minutes, you'll all be dead."

"That guess is premature."

A new voice.

Male.

Coming from the shadows.

Leandra startled, tried to see who was back there, but had no luck in the dimness.

Another vampire? Couldn't be. The timbre of the voice didn't have the hollow quality of the vampires.

"Lucia," the voice said. "You come to New Orleans and never say hi. You come to my restaurant and never stop by to check on me."

Leandra glanced at her aunt.

Lucia's eyes glowed almost white. Her mouth was open in a perfect letter o. "Quake."

"At your service."

The bushes parted, and out stepped the tallest, blondest man Leandra had ever seen. His long hair was pulled back into a ponytail. His features were Nordic, high cheekbones, bird of prey eyes in a shade of blue that brought images of summer to mind.

He kept his gaze on Lucia, stepping closer until they were standing next to each other.

The air between them almost seemed to crackle with energy.

"You—" Lucia's tongue seemed to have frozen.

The old vampire stepped back. "It can't be. You're not… You're dead. You died more than a hundred years ago."

Quake pinched a muscular forearm peeking out from rolled up long sleeves. "Hardly dead."

"This can't be." The old vampire was flustered, his hands shaking as he raised them to nervously push back hair that hadn't moved out of place.

Quake's eyes narrowed to slits, his hand moved, so quickly Leandra wasn't sure she'd seen it move.

Then, as if there had been seismic activity, a deep rumble came from the ground beneath the vampires, a rift erupted, creating a chasm.

And just like that—

No vampires.

"Now. Where were we?" Quake turned to Leandra. "It's nice to finally make your acquaintance, since your aunt clearly has no interest in introducing me to her family. Quaker. I go by Quake. At your service. I'm an old friend of Lucia's."

A coughing fit seized Lucia as she doubled over. When she raised her head, her cheeks were red. "Friend? Is that what we are—were?"

"Hardly enemies," Quake said. "I didn't intend to

disrupt your family reunion. I was on the way out when I received word there was trouble brewing."

And again, with a speed that made shifters seem to move as slow as a sloth, Quake was gone.

"That's Quake?" Leandra couldn't think of anything else to say. She was shell-shocked.

First the vampires.

Then Theo finding out about the baby.

Then the vampires were gone—just like that —vanquished.

Then this was the infamous Quake.

"That's Quake." Lucia turned toward the path. "Let's get you home. And I'm sure you two have a few things to discuss."

Meaning she doesn't want to talk about him—it.

The Cabin at Arceneaux Point

LEANDRA LAY next to the man she'd pledge her life to. She was ready to do exactly that. A growling sound came from deep within Theo's chest. It was his lion.

Leandra nodded, placing her hand on his hardness.

Moisture pooled between her legs. Her desire for him seeped into her panties then trailed between her thighs.

She pushed him backward, seating him on the bed, and raised her dress to her hips.

Theo's pupils dilated, and his lion's presence glowed in the depths of his eyes. He took her hand and pulled her onto his lap, straddling him.

"I want to bond."

He'd asked her several times; she didn't know why they hadn't yet.

"Are you sure?" His eyes penetrated her, seeking the answers within.

"I'm yours. There is no doubt. We should make it official."

He groaned, pushed her dress aside, sliding into her with a powerful plunge.

She gasped, the sound torn from her. She felt him deep, so very deep, his thickness stretching her as if he were holding her from the inside.

She arched her body, head thrown back, enthralled by her lion-shifter man.

His lips pressed against her neck, his tongue traveling upward to her chin then downward.

Leandra wrapped her legs around his waist, pulling him deeper inside, sheathing him fully. His fingers dug into the flesh of her ass, pulling her closer, then pushing her off while he drove in relentlessly.

Her body was on fire from the barrage of pleasure from every plunge he made into her.

She felt a scream building up in her, but had no power to control it. It started as a low moan that was building toward crescendo. He drove into her over and over while her moans grew with the ferocity of every drive.

It didn't take long. They were both still driven by the adrenaline of the evening's events. With a final climax that seized control of her body, she stiffened as aftershock followed aftershock.

He pulled her close and latched onto her, sinking canines into the spot where her neck met her shoulder.

Her gasp gave away the burning pain of his bite. With a long swipe of his tongue, he licked the blood seeping from the puncture wounds. The impression changed from pain to a summit of desire as he bonded her.

His thrusts grew stronger, more insistent, he drove into her with a ferocity, the whole time releasing himself deep inside.

Theo kissed her lips, allowing her to taste the iron flavor of her blood.

She lay her head on his chest. "I'm sorry I didn't tell you about the baby sooner. I wanted to be sure she'd be okay."

"You witches and your ways." His voice held forgiveness. "We should pick a name."

"I have thoughts," Leandra offered hesitantly.

"Do tell." There was a smile in his tone.

"Phoebe Latrice."

"After my mother, and your Mémé."

She nodded against his chest.

"I love it."

Leandra looked up, her eyes brimming with tears. "Truly?"

"Truly." Theo's strong jawline, the earnest mouth, the planes that divulged his Mediterranean heritage, they gave away his emotions. "Phoebe Latrice. She'll be the most amazing shifter witch ever."

"Witch shifter," Leandra teased.

Theo laughed. "And her godmother will be Lucia."

Leandra joined him in laughter. "How about Quake as a godfather?"

"Lucia will kill you." Theo's smile was mischievous. "Let's do it."

"I think I'd like to have Quake in our family."

"Agreed." Theo nodded. "I'd rather have him on my side than against me."

"Mm-hmm," Leandra made a sound of assent. "I had a thought though." It had just come to her. "Lézare should be a godfather, too."

"You're sure?" Theo frowned. "I don't want you doing something that makes you uncomfortable."

"I like the Arceneaux, and, knowing them like I

do now…" Leandra nodded. "I think our fates are permanently intertwined."

"You're an amazing woman, Leandra Mathieu."

"And you, Theodoros Ricoletti, son of an Italian lion shifter and a Greek woman, are one of a kind."

Theo planted a kiss on the tip of her nose. "I'm your kind."

"That you are."

"Forever."

"And then some."

KEEP READING for an excerpt from the next Shifters Forever Worlds book!

Who wants to be immortal in a land where death feels like the only true escape?

Étienne Arceneaux. Ancestor of Lézare. Released from the bonds of slavery by death. Only this was not the death any man would have wanted. The only remedy to avoiding that death was the last one he would have wanted.

Except Étienne wasn't given a choice. The high witch of Black Glade Coven, Latrice Mathieu knew that he would play an important role in the future of the New Orleans supernatural society.

She never knew how much.

See a side of Leandra Mathieu's grandmother Latrice you couldn't have imagined. She travels north after the Civil War to take her white tiger shifter daughter Lucia to the man who fathered her. Only to lose her.

Follow Étienne on his path to freedom, and then take Étienne's sojourn back to Arceneaux plantation, the place he'd never thought he'd return to, where he meets Celine Arceneaux, a redheaded fiery beauty that claims his heart as fiercely as he claims her body.

Life is not quite so simple for the returned Étienne Arceneaux in the Arceneaux Plantation, a place that put the scars on his soul which are almost as visible as the scars on his body.

Inescapable scars.

Inescapable lives.

Inescapable futures.

Visit ElleThorne.com to sign up for Elle's newsletter!

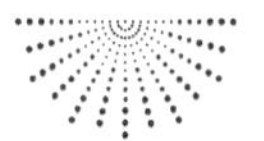

CHAPTER 1

É tienne tiptoed through the darkness, stopping to calm one of the dogs that hung around the slave cabins of Arceneaux Plantation. He petted the dog's head and prayed the others would stay quiet for him this time, like they had all the other times.

He was quiet because there'd be hell to pay if he were caught again where he shouldn't be.

Étienne was no child with a curfew. No, not at all. Étienne was trapped in slavery. Trapped, though he was the son of the plantation owner's son. And yet his birth, and even his very life, had been kept a secret.

His toe hooked on a rebellious tree root, but he regained his step before catapulting and thrown into a headlong fall. A fall wouldn't be a good thing. Not only because he'd get caught and feel the lash of the whip on his shoulders—his flesh hadn't healed from the last time three days ago—no, not just the excruciating touch of the whip, but also the possibility he'd lose the precious cargo he was carrying tonight.

Cargo in the form of honey he was taking to his grandmother, who lived in one of the cabins. Étienne stayed in the quarters with the other single men closer to the main house, though many nights he wished he were still in his grandmother's cabin.

That would never happen. The overseer had a special brand of hatred for Étienne. Maybe it was because his skin was so light. Maybe it was because his heritage was whispered about, if not confirmed. Or maybe it was plain old meanness, as others often said.

The night was dark, the moon barely a sliver, with sounds of the nightlife that surrounded the swampy lands outside the city of New Orleans. Just a few more yards. He stuck close to the trees and cabins, staying in the shadows, his senses on high alert for watchful eyes that could bring hell to him tomorrow morning.

If I'm caught.

Yes, if he were caught. Which he'd do his damnedest not to be.

Finally, he was in front of Nana's door. He raised his hand to scratch on the wood lightly, to make no more noise than a rodent.

The door opened before he could touch it. Nana's beautiful dark face, eyes wide, peered into the darkness. She always opened the door as if she knew he would be there. As if expecting him.

Every time.

Recognition shone in her eyes. They narrowed as she smiled, teeth emerging in a broad grin. "Étienne." Her voice was a mere whisper, not rising above the din of crickets and toads.

Étienne nodded and held up a tiny container. The viscous amber liquid glowed in the candlelight shining behind Nana.

She reached through the crack, a tiny hand on an arm that was thinner than Étienne would have wanted, and she pulled him inside with a strength that belied her age and size.

"Come." She closed the door behind him softly, then whirled on him, arms wrapping around Étienne's waist. "What did you do to get that?" She raised her eyes to his.

It was then he noticed the white hairs coursing through her dark ones at her temples.

It pained Étienne to see his grandmother with signs of age, and the signs grew more and more prevalent with every visit he paid her.

Truth was, Nana, known to everyone else as Marguerite, was more than his grandmother. Nana had raised him from birth.

Étienne squeezed her shoulders, not too tightly, bearing in mind her frailty, then placed the prized cargo into her palm.

"You'll stay. Let me get you something warm to drink." She winked at him conspiratorially. "I have tea grounds."

"And how did you get those?" Étienne smiled at the sheer joy on her face.

"I have my ways. And the hot water is ready."

The hot water always was ready. Nana kept water heating all hours of the day. She never knew when she'd be called on to make a poultice or boil herbs. Everyone came to Nana for healing.

Moments later, Étienne was sitting at her table made of rummaged lumber, on a chair made of more rummaged lumber, his feet digging into the dirt floor.

Nana put a biscuit before him, a layer of the honey he'd just brought slathered liberally on each half.

"No, Nana. You eat."

"Don't be silly." She showed him two more biscuits in a basket under a rag.

Étienne took a bite, knowing it gave her pleasure to watch him eat. He followed the bite with a swallow of the hot tea. She'd put honey in there, too.

Nana sat across from him. "There's blood on your back."

He winced. Not from the physical pain, but from Nana knowing what he'd been through.

"Too bad Old Mister Arceneaux doesn't know the ways of his new overseer."

It's not like he really knew the ways of the old one either. Étienne only shrugged, causing himself pain. But he resisted the urge to flinch when he moved forward. The lashes he'd taken the other day did more than smart.

Étienne's mother had died in childbirth, and when asked, Nana had claimed to all that did not need to know that her newborn had died, too. Nana raised Étienne as her own. She wouldn't have managed this if she hadn't been so trusted, and not kept under close watch. Old Mister Arceneaux—as she called him—had a special fondness for her.

The man who Étienne resembled, his father Phillip—Young Mister Arceneaux—though no one would say so out loud, had left to go to college, his long forgotten tryst with Étienne's mother had remained as such—forgotten.

As well as the child they'd had. When Phillip had come home for break, he'd asked about Étienne's mother, thinking maybe one day they could have something, move far away where the scourge of slavery did not taint their lives, but he was told she'd died. And he was never told about the son he'd fathered.

Phillip never came back to the plantation again. Étienne had no knowledge of what his father looked like, no idea of hair color, eye color, the sound of his voice, nothing.

And if he were honest, at this stage in his life, he didn't care. It didn't matter to him that Phillip Arceneaux didn't know he existed. What did matter was his mother died giving birth to him, and Phillip Arceneaux wasn't even aware of it.

"I have to go before I'm caught here."

"Go. But…" Nana hesitated. Her fingers worked the rag in her hands, over and over, twisting the threadbare fabric.

Étienne waited patiently for her to start again.

After a deep breath, she did. "I've been visited," Nana said.

He knew what that meant. She'd had a visit from the dark visitor, the one that heralded death. It was said amongst the others that Nana had the gift. The dark visitor would tell her of a death.

"Who now?" Étienne had humored Nana over the years, though to be truthful, he'd found her predictions had been mostly accurate. It was eerie, but he always pushed her gifts aside. Étienne wanted nothing to do with the preternatural or supernatural world. The idea of dark visitors made his skin crawl.

"My turn," Nana said.

He shook his head. "No. You're too young."

And she was, in spirit, though at eighty-something years, her body denied her the privilege of youth.

He kissed her on the cheek. "I'll stop by soon."

If he could.

If he could sneak away.

If he wasn't shackled again.

Why he irked the overseer more than any other on the plantation, Étienne had no idea, but he dealt with it. As best as a man who had no choice and no rights could.

What's next?

Inescapable

Who wants to be immortal in a land where death feels like the only true escape?

Étienne Arceneaux. Ancestor of Lézare. Released from the bonds of slavery by death. Only this was not the death any man would have wanted. The only remedy to avoiding that death was the last one he would have wanted.

Except Étienne wasn't given a choice. The high witch of Black Glade Coven, Latrice Mathieu knew that he would play an important role in the future of the New Orleans supernatural society.

She never knew how much.

See a side of Leandra Mathieu's grandmother Latrice you couldn't have imagined. She travels north after the Civil War to take her white tiger shifter daughter Lucia to the man who fathered her. Only to lose her.

Follow Étienne on his path to freedom, and then take Étienne's sojourn back to Arceneaux plantation, the place he'd never thought he'd return to, where he meets Celine Arceneaux, a redheaded fiery beauty that claims his heart as fiercely as he claims her body.

Life is not quite so simple for the returned Étienne Arceneaux in the Arceneaux Plantation, a place that put the scars on his soul which are almost as visible as the scars on his body.

Inescapable scars.

Inescapable lives.

Inescapable futures.

Please refer to the website for newest releases as we spend time with our Shifters Forever and all the wonderful spin off series!

ElleThorne.com

Thank you for reading!

SHIFTERS FOREVER SERIES

Are you ready for it?

I have a whole world full of shifters to share with you. I'm listing them here, in the suggested reading order, though I've tried to make it so that you can pick up anywhere in the series as we all have probably done that at one point or another.

Many of these are organized in box sets for savings. Be sure to visit www.ellethorne.com to see which box sets are out!

Where's the best place to start? Well, probably with SHIFTERS FOREVER.

SHIFTERS FOREVER

Grizzly bear shifters and their mates steam up the pages in these swoon-worthy paranormal romances. From trespassers with hidden agendas to curvaceous women who are ready to take a chance, the stories in this collection will capture your heart.

- PROTECTION
- SEDUCTION
- PERSUASION
- INVITATION
- TEMPTATION
- ATTRACTION

ALWAYS AFTER DARK

A spinoff with the white tiger from Shifters Forever: Vax, born Vittorio Tiero. He's the one that helped Kane out during a shifter battle. Follow the Tiero family, a group of white tiger shifters, as they head to America to find love... and heart-stopping danger. Full of romance, suspense, and gritty drama, this red-hot collection is sure to entertain!

- CONTROVERSY
- TERRITORY
- ADVERSARY
- SANCTUARY

NEVER AFTER DARK

Another spinoff that takes place in Europe. Here we visit cities along the Mediterranean and meet the old school Tiero white tiger shifters who are resistant to change.

- FORBIDDEN
- FORSAKEN
- FORGOTTEN
- FOREPLAY

ONLY AFTER DARK

Taking place in New Orleans, the Arceneaux shifters, led by Lézare, Vax's white tiger cousin—on his mother's side—are sure to capture your hearts. The Arceneaux are the black sheep of the family. Lézare doesn't cave to public opinion. He dictates policy in the area he rules and he shuns old school European rules and regimes.

- DESIRABLE
- INSATIABLE
- COMBUSTIBLE
- UNDENIABLE
- INEVITABLE
- INESCAPABLE

BITTER FALLS FOREVER

This romance features Mae Forester's nephew Dane Forester, a freewheeling, sexy, successful, movie star who uses every role and every woman to escape and forget the heartbreak he left in Bitter Falls.

• UNBOUND

BARELY AFTER DARK

This series features more of Mae Forester's nephews! Grizzly bear shifters steam up the pages in these swoon-worthy paranormal romances. From trespassers with hidden agendas to curvaceous women who are ready to take a chance, the stories in this collection will capture your heart.

• CROSS
• LANCE
• JUDGE

EVER AFTER DARK

Get ready to be introduced to the white tigers you learned to love in Always After Dark, Never After Dark, and Only After Dark. See their heritage. Visit

Giovanni Tiero and his brothers Federico and Tito.
Get reacquainted with Isabel Tiero and meet her
sister Capriana Valenti.

- STONEBOUND
- FORMIDABLE

SHIFTERS FOREVER AFTER

This series follows a group of polar bears in New
York. Russian and rumored to be mobbed up, they
are a powerhouse of shifters, determining the fate of
many on the East Coast. Mikhail Romanoff, Layla's
father, runs this outfit with an iron fist. Layla's sexy
cousin Malachi features prominently in this series.

- COMPLICATION
- FASCINATION
- MOTIVATION
- CAPTIVATION
- FLIRTATION
- INFATUATION

FOREVER AFTER DARK

A series which takes place in Denver, Colorado.
Enter a world of secrets and forbidden love. Panther
shifters who who share their worlds with elementals

must decide who they can trust—and who they can't live without.

- NOTORIOUS
- SCANDALOUS
- DELICIOUS
- PERILOUS

SHIFTERS FOREVER MORE Grizzly bear shifters, dragon shifters, sorceresses, elementals, and all types of other paranormal beings and their mates steam up the pages as the Bear Canyon Valley clan sorts through trespassers with hidden agenda, hidden military compounds, top secret experiments and curvaceous women who are ready to take a chance. The romances in this collection will capture your heart and leave your head spinning!

- CONFUSION
- DECISION
- POSSESSION
- ILLUSION
- PASSION
- IMPRESSION

FINALLY AFTER DARK

Follow a pack of dire wolves as they encounter Valkyrie and Berserkers and determine the origins of their kind throughout the ages, while discovering their fated mates.

- ORIGINS
- CHALLENGE
- DAMAGE
- RAVAGE
- MORE TO FOLLOW!

I do hope you'll be able to join me on this wonderful journey with our Shifters Forever Worlds Shifters and their mates!

To receive exclusive updates from Elle Thorne and to be the first to get your hands on the next release, please sign up for her mailing list.

Elle Thorne Newsletter

If you can't click, just put this in your browser: http://www.ellethorne.com/contact

MY PERSONAL GUARANTEE:

THIS WILL ONLY BE USED TO ANNOUNCE NEW RELEASES AND SPECIALS. AND TO GIVE MY WONDERFUL SPECIAL READERS A LITTLE GIFT.

SHIFTERS REALMS

I have another new world of shifters! How exciting! I can't wait to share them with you!

Be sure to visit www.ellethorne.com to see which ones are out!

Where's the best place to start? Here we go!

IRON FLATS

Wolf shifters and their mates steam up the pages in these paranormal romances. From rovers with hidden agendas to women who are ready to take a chance, to unknown the stories in this collection will capture your heart.

- IRON FLATS EXILE
- IRON FLATS JUSTICE
- IRON FLATS REBEL
- IRON FLATS MAVERICK

MORE TO FOLLOW!

I do hope you'll be able to join me on this wonderful journey with our Shifters Forever Worlds Shifters and their mates!

To receive exclusive updates from Elle Thorne and to be the first to get your hands on the next release, please sign up for her mailing list.

Elle Thorne Newsletter

If you can't click, just put this in your browser: http://www.ellethorne.com/contact

MY PERSONAL GUARANTEE:
THIS WILL ONLY BE USED TO ANNOUNCE NEW RELEASES AND SPECIALS. AND TO GIVE MY WONDERFUL SPECIAL READERS A LITTLE GIFT.

Shifters Forever Worlds

Shifter Realms

For sales and news, sign up for the newsletter! Thank you for purchasing and downloading my book. Words can't express what it means to me. If you enjoyed this read, please remember to take a second to leave a review. I'd love to know what your favorite parts were.

The fun isn't about to stop. Make sure you sign up for the link to the newsletter.

Hearing from you means the world to me. This would not be possible without you and your love for reading.

With much gratitude, I thank you!

It took Elle Thorne years to stop being a closet romantic.

Originally from Europe, she wouldn't dream of living anywhere else but Texas. Unless it was another southern—translation: warm!—state. A southern European by birth, she wants to be near the water and the Mediterranean temperatures if possible.

Where does she like to hang out? Near a lake, a beach, preferably with a latte—extra shot of espresso, please! She's inspired by the everyday men who make dreams come true. She loves a roughneck, especially one with a callous or two on his hands. A man who knows how to fix a car, please a woman, and protect what's his.

Nothing less will do.

To receive exclusive updates from Elle Thorne and to be the first to get your hands on the next release, please sign up for her mailing list.
Put this in your browser:
www.ellethorne.com/contact

My personal guarantee:
This will only be used to announce new releases and specials. And to give my wonderful special readers a little gift.